Charles Henry Robbins

The Gam

Whaling Stories

Charles Henry Robbins

The Gam
Whaling Stories

ISBN/EAN: 9783743367043

Manufactured in Europe, USA, Canada, Australia, Japa

Cover: Foto ©Andreas Hilbeck / pixelio.de

Manufactured and distributed by brebook publishing software (www.brebook.com)

Charles Henry Robbins

The Gam

THE GAM,

BEING A GROUP OF WHALING STORIES

BY

CAPT. CHARLES HENRY ROBBINS,

WHO GRATEFULLY ACKNOWLEDGES THE EDITORIAL
SUGGESTIONS OF HIS FRIEND,
MR. ROLLIN LYNDE HARTT.

NEW BEDFORD:
H. S. HUTCHINSON & COMPANY.
1899.

R. H. Blodgett & Co., Printers,
30 Bromfield St., Boston.

INTRODUCTION.

I HAVE for many years wondered that the romantic and exciting experiences of the whale fishery have not been preserved more often in records in our literature. Occasionally we have had sketches of one or another detail in this marvellous adventure. But it would seem as if the brave men who engage in such adventure handle harpoons more willingly than they handle pens. And so you shall hear many a story of such adventure told by men who speak of what they have seen, while you do not read one such story. I was very glad, therefore, to hear that Capt. Charles H. Robbins had put to paper some accounts of his own earlier experiences, and I am very glad that he has been persuaded to publish them. I am glad to say to any friend of mine that he may place confident reliance on the narrative of Capt. Robbins, as being that of one who tells of what he saw, of which indeed he was much himself.

EDWARD E. HALE.

Roxbury, May 27, 1899.

CONTENTS.

ILLUSTRATIONS.

THE FATTED CALF.

"There's many a slip 'twixt the two mugs!"
— *O'Hoolihan's Proverbs.*

"Not by any means," said the Girl. "On the other hand, you are very vividly remembered!"

"And by what?"

"By lots of things — glorious things, too — but I hardly think you're proud of them now!"

"Oh! I don't know."

"I do, though," said a voice from across the supper table. "He's as proud of them as ever he was. Five years haven't changed him a particle. He's just the same incorrigible young rascal he was before he went away to sea!"

"Is that true?" said the Girl.

"I'm afraid it is," he laughed, "I'm truly afraid it is! Just ask the 'old man.' He'll tell you. But" — the jolly prodigal turned to the Girl at his side. He blushed as her eyes met his. It was so long since he had talked to girls. He felt like a tough, old right whale addressing a little pink water-lily.

"But," he made bold to ask, "what are the 'glorious' things you think I'm not proud of?"

" Mr. Robbins, if you please, I prefer not to tell." She tossed her pretty head, and the two long, dark ringlets, nestling against her soft cheeks, seemed to laugh and taunt him. They were as bewitchingly mischievous as her brown eyes, or the dimples that came and went with her smiles, or even that defiant little toss of her head. The tiny gold beads, too, and the big cameo brooch were leagued together against him. So were her smooth, white shoulders. For in those good old days of Forty-one, the Girl, whose picture (in daguerrotype, of course) is still considered the supreme triumph of New Bedford photography, was in the first bloom of her youth and beauty.

" Oh, but you're not going to get off so easy! " said still another voice. " If Dorothy won't tell, *we will.* You're remembered for putting a flat stone on the top of Daddy Jones's chimney. Yes, and for smoking old Daddy out of his cobbler-shop as if he'd been a poor hunted wood-chuck."

"And for writing a Bible verse on Daddy Jones's door," cried a lad with a rose in his coat, trying to loom into view from the lee side of a much-hewn turkey. " Don't you remember? It was when Daddy had got so lazy he never opened his shop till ten in the morning, and the Prodigal and I wrote on his door, "*He is not dead, but sleepeth!*"

"Yes, yes," cried the blonde girl in lavendar, "for that, too, and for kicking the football against Squire Tomlinson's window so he came out as mad as a March hare, and seized the ball and put it in the stove. O, we remember you well! The deeds that New Bedford boys do live after them. Besides, we've not forgotten how you got another foot-ball next day and filled it with gunpowder, and then kicked that against the window till the Squire came and caught it and put it in the stove just like the first one, and then there wasn't any stove."

The Prodigal turned again to Dorothy. "You wouldn't have told those stories, *would* you?" He thought this tentative sally a triumph of pure heroism. He was never so timid in his life. He had chased whales and darted harpoons into their slippery black backs out of the dancing prow of a whale-boat; he had gone among tattooed natives who might have cooked and eaten him had they chosen; he had clambered down over the ship's bows in a storm to repair a broken bob-stay, and had stuck it out bravely till the bob-stay was mended, though he was plunged twenty times under water before the process was complete; but those exploits were as nothing beside this highly problematic encounter with ringlets, and dimples, and soft eyes, and tender white shoulders!

" No, sir," said Dorothy (that was before young
people were taught never to say 'sir' to anybody)
" I assure you I wouldn't have told those stories;
tortures couldn't have drawn them from me!"

The Prodigal felt thirty feet tall. Dorothy's
smile made his heart leap. It was like Words-
worth's rainbow in its effect.

" But," said Dorothy, growing stern all of a
sudden, " I expect to be rewarded for my good-
ness. I've got you in my power now, and you
must do my bidding to the death!" (She looked
straight through him with her round eyes.) " And
I greatly fear you'll fail of your quest; and if you
do fail, then you're no true knight!" (Dimpling
again, her pretty cheeks coming up ever so little
to make her eyes dance and sparkle.) "Wretched
swain," (very serious again, pausing, with tight-
closed lips), " I command you to confess all your
manifold sins and wickednesses — yes, every one
of them. Every jolly wrong thing you did while
you served as cabin boy on the dear old *Swift*,
and if the sins you confess aren't as picturesque as
those you committed in New Bedford before you
turned whaleman, then" (a majestic toss of
the head that set the ringlets caressing her
pink cheeks again) "I'll refuse to grant you
absolution!"

" Yes, old fellow, you'll do as Dorothy says, if you're wise. She has her way sooner or later every time and there's no escape. We all have to submit, and you're no exception, even if you *are* a whaleman !"

Submit ? Of course he would submit. He would have pushed a holy stone up and down the deck from morn till dewy eve (and never growled) if the Girl had bidden him. He would have tarred the rigging from the fore-royal stay to the topping-lift (and left no " holidays ") if the Girl had so ordered. He would have slushed the mast in the blaze of the torrid equatorial sun (and without inwardly cursing the lot of poor Jack) if Dorothy's dimpling smiles would have approved his toil. And, as the greater includes the less, he was ready to tell at her behest how he had consti-tuted himself a *persona non grata* aboard the whale-ship *Swift.*

He was twenty. At fifteen he had signed sail-ing papers that bound him away as a cabin-boy on a three years' voyage sperm-whaling, but the three years had stretched out to four, and the four to nearly five. At last he was home again, after roving so long among the islands of the South Pacific. He had just arrived. In fact, twenty-four hours had not yet gone by since he

THE GAM.

had rushed in upon his mother and been formally introduced to his own sisters, who had grown to unrecognizable dimensions since his departure; and this grand New England banquet was being given in his honor by neighbors just over the way. The sixteen young people around the table were his old schoolmates. They called him the Prodigal; but well they knew that the boy had come home unstained from his wanderings. With equal pertinence, and not less, they called the turkey a "fatted calf."

He had perhaps an unusually pleasant way of telling a story, this young sea-rover — a way that has remained with him until this day. He hoists his Blue Peter, heaves up his mud-hook, shakes out his canvas and puts to sea. Nobody tries to help him. He sails over his course as straight as a well-found ship, and he comes into port with a new coat of paint, and pendant flying.

"Well," said the Prodigal, "if I must, I must. And I'll begin by telling you how the old man put his watch in soak."

"Stop!" cried the Girl. "I object. This is not to be a story about an old gentleman. What's more, it's not to be told in sailor language. It's to be about yourself" (such a sweet tone as she said "yourself") "and it's to be told in faultless

New Bedford English (eyes again, utterly distracting) or I'll — ! "

" But," the Prodigal answered, " you've not yet heard the story. Listen. The ' old man ' is the captain (they always call him so on shipboard); ' putting one's watch in soak ' is not a sea-term at all ; and the story is really about *me*, and it's told in the only language I know, for I've lived in the cabin like a fine gentleman. You must remember that the boy's not allowed to go before the mast.

" So, here goes." He was now under way. He would forge ahead, all fluking, without further interruption.

" After we'd been about six months out from home, we anchored at Porter's, one of the Gallapagos Islands, and there we found an old apple-bowed, square-sterned, painted-ported bark, the *Surprise*, of Wilmington, Cap'n Crocker. Next morning the two old men — Crocker and my own cap'n — gave liberty on shore for all hands, except cooks, stewards, and boys, to hunt terrapin, if you call that liberty. After they had landed, the old man and Crocker called us boys and took us ashore to help them try and catch a seal. Mighty glad we were to go.

" We landed on a little island, only three miles round and covered with woods. It was high and very rugged.

"The cap'ns gave us youngsters leave to ramble about for an hour, so we thought we'd cross the island, get down to the shore on the other side, and follow the beach back to the boat. We had high hopes of finding a seal. for neither of us had ever seen one alive.

"It was easy enough getting to the top of the island, but from there on it was all a tangle of gullies and ravines, and when we finally came to the other side we found ourselves looking down from the edge of a three-hundred-foot cliff. It made us dizzy, as you may imagine, to peer over it, but we lay out flat on our stomachs and rested our heads on our hands and our elbows on the rocks, and studied that bluff. It was straight up and down, like the *Swift's* checkered sides. There was no beach at the bottom. There was a dead flat calm, no waves at all save the everlasting heave and swell that never ceased and never *will* cease; and yet the breakers were white at the foot of the cliff and we could hear their roar. It was what we sailors call an iron-bound coast.

"Our hearts went down into the soles of our boots. Climb down that precipice? Crawl along at the water's edge? Not by a jugful!

" Suddenly it occured to us we must have been gone a pretty long hour. So we started back — disappointed and scared and ashamed — the way we had come, as well as we could judge, and we were not far wrong. But everything was against us. Thorns and brambles caught us, one or both. Steep crags got in our way on purpose. Gullies sank under our feet. So fully four hours had gone by when we came in view of the landing place again. The cap'ns were hallooing with all their might, but we were too scared to answer and so kept still. That didn't pay, though. When the old man clapped his eyes on me, he hollered out at the top of his lungs, ' Come here, you rascal. I'll learn you to run away ! I'll learn you to keep me waiting ! Come here till 1 make a little spread-eaglet of you ! *I'll* learn you this lesson so it'll stick in your back as well as your head ! Come ! Are you dead ? Show a leg there ! '

" With that the old man grabbed hold of the boat's warp and was going to give me a thrashing with the bitter end of it. But the other cap'n begged me off.

" ' Well,' said the old man, ' I'll put *druggs* on the rascal so he won't run out so blamed swift. Here's what *I'll* do. Cap'n Crocker can have his way about the little spread-eaglet, but *I'll* have *mine* about that twenty-pound stone over yonder there. Come, sonnywax, bring me that flat stone —that big, round one, with the barnacles all over it!'

"I went and brought the stone. It was shaped like Daddy Jones's lapstone and it weighed not an ounce under twenty pounds. The old tyrant took that stone and slung it to my back with a strong cord slipped round in a lark's head knot.

"'Now,' he roared, 'I guess you'll not get out of hailing distance again this cruise!'

"Then we pushed the boat off through the rollers and made for the large island. I tugged at my oar with the big stone banging against my shoulder-blades and jabbing the barnacles into my back. I would rather have taken the rope-ending.

"I thought we'd never get ashore, but at last we did. We rushed the boat out of the water on a fine sand beach, a mile or more long and as straight as a street.

"The cap'ns started ahead, keeping a bright lookout for seals, but we boys lagged behind, and as soon as we dared we got a new stone, the same shape but only about half as heavy, and no barnacles on it, and we put it in place of the twenty-pounder on my back. I tell you, it was a relief!

" The cap'ns had got a long way in the lead —
a quarter of a mile at the very least — when suddenly I heard a rifle-shot and saw a moving puff
of blue smoke.

" The old man had shot a seal, and the wounded
beast was dancing around the beach like a man in
a sack-race, and every jump he made brought him
a little nearer the water.

" The old man wanted me now as he'd never
wanted me before, for I had the powder and balls
in my pocket to reload his rifle.   He hollered like
mad.

" ' Hurry up, you scoundrel!   Do you hear ?
Quick!   Drop your ballast, I tell you ; quick, or
I'll *thrash* you!   Quick I say !   *Quick !*   QUICK !!
QUICK ! ! ! '

" I ran as fast as I could, but the sand was soft
and the stone was hard and I made sorry work
of it.

" The old man chased the seal into the water
with a club, but as soon as the animal got afloat
in the surf he was the better off for the change.
He dashed away for life and liberty — the old
man after him, dealing murderous blows with the
cudgel.   As I came up, puffing and blowing like a
winded walrus, the old man was in up to his ears
in salt water and the seal was bleeding from a

dozen gashes at once. Another swing of the club put him out of his misery.

"The old man came splashing and sputtering out of the surf, dragging his lifeless prey after him.

"'Blast the boy,' he yelled, 'I've got a pretty drenching.'

"Cap'n Crocker roared with laughter. 'Better have left the boy free to run, sir!'

"The old man shook himself like a wet dog.

"'Cap'n,' cried Crocker, rolling from side to side with amusement, 'can you tell me the time o' day?'

"The old man felt for his watch, only to discover that he had ruined it in the surf!

"Crocker stamped about the beach, bellowing like a facetious big bull. 'O-ho-ho!' he howled, I've seen many a beautiful timepiece go in soak in my day, but never before on account of a rascally cabin boy with a stone on his back!'

"So that's how the old man put his watch in soak, your majesty. Please, may I stop now?"

He looked into Dorothy's eyes as he spoke. They looked into his. There was nothing remarkable in that, but nevertheless he felt as if he had taken something that didn't belong to him. However, he had no desire to put it back.

"*Absolvo te!*" said the Girl. "Isn't that what
they say at confessional!" A burst of generous
laughter shook the table.

"What did we tell you?" said he of the red
rose. "Just the same rogue as before he turned
blubber-hunter. Daddy Jones was right. You
remember he said, 'Glad he's gone — *pesky* glad,
but I pity that there cap'n o' his'n!'"

Turkey, doughnuts, mince-pie, and sweet cider
had found their way to destruction. The merry
party left the table and trooped into the large,
old-fashioned parlor, where the fun began afresh.
There was dancing, in the quaint manner now
gone by; there were games, of the hilarious
sort no longer in vogue; there were songs
— forgotten, most of them, long ere this. The
Prodigal thought it a sumptuous occasion. For
five years he had not sat in a cushioned chair
or stepped upon a carpeted floor. To his sailorly
eyes that staid and demure parlor, with its tall
looking-glasses, its marbled wall-paper, and its
solemn, mahogany furniture, was princely mag-
nificence. To all intents it far outshone the
wealth of Ormus and of Ind.

But the Girl was there — not always at his side,
but always responsive. Even if she sat, for the
moment, at the farther end of the room, under

the silver candalabra, she made him feel that her
interest was in him. Was it her eyes? Perhaps
— for they were always brightest as they met his.
Or was it her pretty posture? Very likely — for
it was always one of eager attention when he
spoke. He thought for a moment that he was
being mischievously pursued. Then he thought
it rather nice to be pursued. Finally he thought
the Girl was not at all to blame for pursuing so
interesting a person as the returned Prodigal from
the South Pacific. Besides, had not he done all
he knew how, in his sailorly way, to interest the
Girl?

"You didn't do as you promised," she said,
when they chanced to come side by side again.
"You promised to confess all your sins, and you
stopped with one — though it was a very good
one. And now, sir, if you don't confess another
this very minute if not sooner, I'll excommunicate you!"

"How's that done?"

"You'll find out to your grief," said the red
rose, "if you don't tell another story as good as
the last, and that immediately."

"Yes, yes," they all cried, "confess your sins
or we'll excommunicate you, too, and it'll be
something awful — awful!"

They drew their chairs close around the Prodigal. There was no way of escape. He was
secretly glad there was none.

Doubtless it was not wholly by accident that
Dorothy sat directly in front of him. Her seat
was a sort of low hassock. She curled herself
round it prettily, one knee raised, one little slipper
peeping out from the edge of her yellow satin
gown, her hands clasped over her knee, and her
sweet face lifted up toward his. A girl is her
loveliest when she looks up. Probably that is
why Dorothy had chosen the hassock.

"Well, if I must, I must. This time I'll tell
you about the Ten Commandments.

"One Sunday, not so very long after the old
man had put his watch in soak, I happened to be
feeling a bit out of sorts. I knew that if I told
the old man I was sick he'd dose me with castor
oil every hour for a week. So I cast about for a
nice, quiet place to lie down and go to sleep. I
found just what I wanted and, willingly running
the risk of punishment, I curled myself up in the
second mate's bunk and sailed for the land of Nod.

"Now it was my duty to take the hog-yoke on
deck at eleven o'clock." (Dorothy's eyes said,
"What, sir, do you mean by a hog-yoke?")
"That's the quadrant, you know, for the old man

to shoot the sun" (a frown of perplexity on Dorothy's white forehead) — " I mean, for the old man to take the sun's altitude and see what latitude we were in. That's the only safe way to steer a ship, you know.

"But that day the quadrant didn't come on deck in time. In fact, it didn't come at all.

" The old man was frantic. He set all hands searching for me. They hunted in the cabin, they hunted in the fo'c'sle — that's where the sailors live, you know ; you call it ' forecastle,' and that's wrong — and they hunted in the steerage ; but nobody could find me.

" Then the old man got anxious. He hailed the men at the mast-heads — wanted to know if they'd seen anything floating on the water astern of the ship, which meant, of course, had the cabin boy gone overboard ? At last the old man got so worried he wasn't content with ordering other folks to hunt, but even turned to and hunted for me himself.

" Now all this while I was dreaming of an enchanted island, loaded with treasures, and I was just going to be married to the queen of the island, when there came a tremendous yank at my collar, and the old man landed me on the floor with a shock that all but shivered my timbers and

2

studded the ceiling with all the blazing stars in creation.

"The old man kicked me up the cabin stairway and gave me half an hour to think. Meanwhile, he was thinking, I knew that. He was inventing some wonderful new kind of punishment, and he was going to try it on me as soon as he'd got it all invented.

"At last he came on deck. 'Boy,' he shouted, 'can you say the Ten Commandments?'

"'No, sir,' I answered. 'I used to when I was in Sunday school, but I can't now, sir.'

"'Then you just tumble down the cabin stairs and bring the Bible on deck.'

"I did as the old man said, and then he gave me the funniest order you ever heard on a ship. 'Go out on the end o' that spanker-boom, take that Bible along with you, and don't you dare to come back till you can say the Ten Commandments from beginning to end without a single mistake, or I'll make a little spread eaglet of you! *That's* what I'll do!'

"What? Don't know what the spanker-boom is? Why, it's the big round spar that keeps the spanker down, and the spanker, you know, is the monstrous hind sail of the ship. *What* a place to learn the Ten Commandments by heart! That spanker-boom is the unsteadiest piece of stick aboard any vessel, and the further out you go the livelier it swings.

"Well, I tucked the book under my left arm, and crawled along that swinging boom, way out over the hurricane house and far beyond the ship's stern. When I got to the end of it, I leaned my breast against the topping-lift, with one arm curled round it, and laced my legs together under the boom.

"Then I began a hunt for the Ten Commandments. I hadn't the faintest notion where to look for them. First I thought I'd try Revelation. Next it seemed more likely they'd turn up somewhere in Ruth. Again, I had an impulse that led me toward Jonah. Jonah is a very popular book among sailors. It's almost as good as the story of Paul's shipwreck, where they put hawsers round and round the ship, just as if they were strapping a trunk.

"But at last I concluded to begin at the first chapter of Genesis, and eat along to windward till I raised the Ten Commandments. Happy thought! I found them in fifteen minutes. Then I set about learning them.

"The boom swung in the wind, the topping-lift quivered from the strain on it, the white wake ran bubbling under me, and the wind blew the pages of the Bible so I thought it would tear them out and whisk them away. Now and then I would look up. Every man on deck was staring aft and wondered what in the name of hemp and oakum the old man had sent the boy out there for!

"As soon as I got the Commandments so I could say them, I crawled back on deck and said my piece to the old man — every word right. The old man told me 'not to forget 'em, for if I did he'd learn 'em into my back with a rope's end so they'd *never* come out.'

"Several Sundays later, instead of giving the crew a day of comparative rest, the old man found them some extra work to do. He conformed to the spirit of the old rhyme,

" ' Six days shalt thou work and do all thou art able,
And on the seventh, holy-stone the deck and clean-scrape the cable.'

But the particular application he gave it was, — having an old torn sail got on deck and mended. The crew were growling as they went about their task. They were as sullen as a crowd of schoolboys kept in at recess.

"I thought I'd see if I could change that a little. So when the old man came on deck, I

strolled past him, muttering just loud enough for
him to hear : 'Remember–the–Sabbath–day–to
keep–it–holy–six–days–shalt–thou–labor– and – do
all–thy–work–but – the – seventh–day–is–the–Sabbath–of–the–Lord–thy–God–in–it–thou–shalt– not
do–any–work–thou–nor–thy–mate – nor – thy–second – mate – nor – thy – third– mate–nor–thy–crew
nor–thy–cook–nor–thy–carpenter–nor–thy–cooper
nor–thy–cabin–boy.'

"The old man pretended he didn't hear me, but
after awhile he went below and I heard his bell ring.

"So down I tumbled, and as soon as the old
man got his face straight he said, ' Boy, what day
is this ? '

" ' Sunday, sir.'

" ' That so ? Then you go straight to the chief
mate and tell him I say knock off work on that
sail and quit breaking the Sabbath day ! '

"After that we used to get a little rest of a
Sunday ; and that's the sum and substance of the
Ten Commandment story. Please may I stop ? "

" *Absolvo te !* " laughed the Girl. Then the
Prodigal suggested a fresh game, and the scene
shifted anew. Instead of a group around the
Prodigal, you had a group around Dorothy.

Now I had all along been thinking—what! *I ?*
Ah, I've let Pussy pop out of my bag of discretion!

Yes, I. A truce to disguises! The Prodigal was myself, or the self that was then — Charlie Robbins, as they all called me — Capn'n Robbins, as they call me today.

To resume (and with an easier conscience) I, Charlie Robbins, cabin-boy, was thinking that Dorothy was the sweetest girl in the world, that I had made a profound impression upon her, and that my life would be an arid waste if I let her escape me. She was so distractingly pretty, and so dangerously clever. I remembered that when I bade her good-bye five years ago she was a year younger than I. Gratifying reflection — she must be so, still!

I was building air-castles.

I knew I must move rapidly. Girls are so different from whales — at least to whalemen. For you get fast to a whale and if he runs, you run; or if he goes down, you wait till he comes up again. Barring accidents, it's only a matter of time till you kill him or he kills you. But with girls its more complicated. Sometimes you're not fast to them when you think you are. Sometimes they go down and never come up again. And when you're a whaleman you've little time for courting. The stay in a home port is shockingly short. That ship in the harbor won't lay her

main yard aback and wait till the chase is ended.
You must be quick.

I made up my mind that I would improve the
first and all subsequent opportunities of charming,
captivating and otherwise hypnotizing this unex-
ampled young lady. Whatever form later chances
might assume, the near and most available one
was my fund of sea-yarns. I was a sort of blubber-
hunting Othello. She was my incomparable
Desdemona.

So I lowered away, every chance I got.

Her taste, I thought, was peculiar. She cared
little or nothing for whales that tossed one's boat
in the air with their flukes, or for the cannibal
islanders that cook one and eat one, or for hurri-
canes and tidal waves and waterspouts and the
terrors of "the vasty deep." She demanded
yarns about *me* (how gratifying!) and about my
"sins." Every time, she would look as grave as
His Holiness of Rome and say, "*Absolvo te!*"
and then laugh — so prettily that I inwardly
cursed myself for ever having adopted the whaleman's lot — and then say, "Go on, Mr. Robbins!
I must have the next story now — and as good
as the last, or I'll excommunicate you!"

They were a curious skein of yarns. How I
was sent to get the grindstone from the locker

under the cabin-stairs, drew out a bag of letters, and in so doing knocked the grindstone against a demijohn of turpentine, which toppled over helplessly, a reeking, jingling wreck, with the consequence that thereafter the old man made me keep a Domesday Book, to record everything I managed to lose or break on board the ship; how I came to be held to blame whenever a tool was mislaid, with the penalty of having to write it in the Book of Judgment, so that by-and-by when I found a lost article I secretly pitched it overboard rather than be blamed for finding it; how, one Sunday morning, the old man took an observation of the sun and gave the data to me to work out the reckoning, but was not pleased with my answer, and accordingly grabbed me by the hair and lifted me clean off the deck, so that I took care to get my hair cut immediately; and when the old man made another observation that afternoon and gave it to me in the same way and with the same result, he grabbed for my hair again and, missing that, lifted me off the deck by my ears, saying he'd "stretch 'em out as long as a jackass!" and this despite the fact that I was right and he was wrong, for we were cruising down the line, and during the night we had crossed the Equator, so that we had to apply our corrections differently ; and also how I stole the cabin molasses keg while we were at Talcuhano, and sold the molasses in a *pulparee* on shore, upon agreement that the empty keg must be brought aboard next evening. But the ship sailed in the morning and both keg and molasses were left behind. Think of the fix that put me in! Presently the steward wanted some molasses for the "doctor" to cook with, — but where in the name of the Great Horned Spoon was that precious molasses keg? Of course I knew nothing about it — absolutely nothing — vastly less than nothing! The men searched everywhere, and the further they searched the madder they got. They swore like great whales. But that was not the worst of it. My conscience swore, too. The thought of lying galled me and cut me, till at last I went to the old man and confessed my crime. That made me feel a whole lot better, but it made the old man feel a whole lot worse! "Blast you, boy, I'll get even with you! You just waltz forward and tell the cooper I say to give you a dozen barrel-staves. I'm going to learn you a lesson that'll last you way over into the next world!" When I came back with the barrel-staves, the old man stationed me in the waist, where everybody on board could watch me, and said, "Now, sonnywax, you take this saw and this plane the carpenter's brought you, and you make a *new* keg to take the place of the one you've stolen. Here's a chance to show your talent. The crew'll come around you and give you *advice* once in a while and *encourage* you, and when the pretty creature's all done they'll hold up their hands and admire it!" I worked four days. At the end of that time I had something in the shape of a keg, but it wouldn't hold water or molasses any more than the "doctor's" cullender. When these four days of atonement were over, the captain told me to quit. I quitted.

How swiftly that pleasant evening ran by! The merry party broke up all too soon, I thought. And yet not too soon. For one reason, at least, I was glad it was over. Now I should see Dorothy home.

It was in the doorway, after the general and particular good-nights, that I asked her if I might.

Oh, tragical deception! The Girl gave me one defiant flash from her brown eyes, and ran like a deer!

That was the last I saw of her.

I went home alone.

Six weeks later I sailed away in the *Balaena*, sperm-whaling again.

THAT GREAT LEVIATHAN.

THE case of Dorothy being now got well out
of the way, I turn, and not without a grateful
sense of relief, to weightier considerations.

For this gam of mine — you know the term?
— is meant to set forth the grave as well as
the trivial interests of that young madcap who
was so early, and withal so auspiciously, put afloat
in the whaling ship *Swift*. It would, in truth,
be far from fair to leave the reader in possession
of the startling revelations of the last chapter,
unless, over against those light and altogether
frivolous narratives, be set some mention of the
serious business of whaling, — its toil, its peril,
its joy and thrill, to say nothing of its magical
fascination for a boy of fifteen.

Pleasantly my memory runs back sixty years to
the day of our departure. Stars and stripes at the
peak, Blue Peter at the fore; officers and crew
on board; four boats on the cranes; and the hold
filled with white oak casks and a stock of provisions to last three years and more; then, as
somebody or other says, "Waiting is what?"

Waiting is the pilot. But, once aboard, his
majesty takes command, and the voyage is begun.

The captain, while the pilot remains in the ship, is a mere inactive looker-on, a person of no more consequence than a passenger or a spare figure-head.

"Mr. Mate, are you all ready?"

"All ready, sir?"

"Then heave ahead!"

"Aye, aye, sir.　Man the windlass!"

Now comes the confusion, the hurrying and blundering, invariably seen on board a ship when she is getting under way with a crew made up largely of green hands; then an attempt on the part of the officers to bring something like order out of this hurly-burly; and while at every turn of the powerful windlass the chain cable rattles heavily on deck, the *Swift* walks steadily up to her anchor as if impatient for the word to spread her white wings and be away.

"A-vast heaving," shouts the first officer.　"A short stay peak, sir!"

"Aye, aye," responds the pilot.

"Let fall and sheet home top-s'ls and to'-gal'n-s'ls!"

Away sprang half a dozen men aloft, and soon the broad sheets of canvas are unfurled and hauled home and the yards are mast-headed.

Next a volley of incomprehensible orders:

" Brace head yards a-starboard ! "

" Lay helm aport ! "

" Heave up the anchor ! "

The first mate answers, " All away, sir ! " and you know then that the good ship has loosed her hold on *terra firma*, and you watch her movements, as — gracefully as a girl in a minuet — she turns her head seaward.

The pilot springs to the bow, now and again shouting his orders to the helmsmen, who invariably echoes the words, that there may be no possibility of mistake.

And so, with a breeze fresh and free, we sped down the bay, borrowing a little, now on one shore, then on the other, or shaving close to some rocky ledge, as our sharp-eyed, skillful guide might direct, in order to shorten our course from the confines of harbor to the freedom of the open sea.

A little farther, and we open up Gay Head lighthouse on the western end of Martha's Vineyard, so called from the abundance of wild grape vines growing there. Once outside, the tiny pilot-boat, which has been dodging about the heavy ship like a will-o'-the-wisp, shoots alongside, and his lordship the pilot and our friends, mostly men of the sea, hasten to make their adieus, and descend to the restless little craft that will soon take them back to their homes. The lingering grasp of hands, the ill-concealed tremor of fare-wells, and the moistened, glistening eye, tell of the friendship of men who have together battled with the giant seas and fierce winds of the Horn, who have stood shoulder to shoulder when short-ening the wings of their hurrying ship in the short-lived gales of the Equator, and who have for long years shared alike in common hardships, joys and sorrows.

The little fairy shoots ahead, and, flying up into the wind, is soon on our weather beam, homeward bound. Three rousing cheers from her deck, and three from the outward bound, and we are alone on the sea, with nothing binding us to the shore but memories of the past and hopes for the future!

And now, indeed, though with everything yet to learn, I was fairly made a sailor of. There was no possible back-wending, however I might thereafterward mope and whimper. Accordingly I turned my heart manfully toward my strange, new life and faced it with earnest cheer.

The first day out, the ship's crew is divided into two watches, larboard and starboard, the former always headed by the first officer and the latter by the second. The men are mustered aft and the rules of the ship laid down to them. At seven that evening, the watch is set, the second officer always taking the first night watch from the home port, and those not on duty go below and sleep — if they can. Next morning all hands are called aft again, this time for choosing boat's crews. The first officer takes precedence by selecting one man, followed in turn by the second, third, and fourth mates, each choosing one, until every boat has a crew standing by her side. Then follows, usually, the emphatic caution, "Now remember to which you belong, and bear a hand when she's called away!"

And what of the voyage? Southward? Yes, in the main; crossing the Gulf Stream; battling, stripped for the fight, with many a heavy gale; passing, with men all the while at our mast-heads, through the "horse latitudes;" lowering our boats, now and then, to give our whalemen practice in rowing; and taking advantage, now, of every slant of wind to press on our way toward the stormy Horn.

Days and long weeks go by, nor are we alone in the tedious struggle. Several sails are in sight, all striving to get south.

And so, with bracing round, or squaring the yards, making and shortening sail, and backing and filling generally, we get a sharp squall, with rain, from the eastward, and then the old salts cast at each other significant glances, which, if rightly interpreted, would say, "I believe we've got the Trades at last!" After a few hours, the wind moderates and hauls to the northward. All sail is set again, with the breeze fresh and free,- and we go bowling along to the southward at the rate of ten knots an hour.

Oh, the beautiful world of waters! Almost every day we pass ships showing the flags of different nations, some near and others in the far distance, all under a press of canvas, and all seeming to revel in the bright sunshine and the breeze. The water, too — so warm and so transparent — is full of life. Porpoises, dolphins, albicore, and barricota are gambolling and sporting in the summer sea. Thousands of birds are on the wing or resting on the waves, while not infrequently a huge fin-back, or sulphur whale rolls lazily along, now throwing clouds of misty spray into the air, and again lashing the water into foam with its broad flukes, doubtless to rid himself of the numerous parasites which persistently strive to fasten themselves upon these worthless vagabonds. Vitality and loveliness are above, beneath and around us, and we seem verily to be sailing on a sea of enchantment. The stars seem nearer, and shine and twinkle with that wonderful brightness seen only in that southern hemisphere. The North star has dipped into the ocean, not to rise again until we cross the Equator on the Pacific ocean. Instead we gaze in novel delight upon the Southern Cross, and we are constantly looking for that mysterious and ghostlike thing known to seamen as the Magellan cloud, and said to mark the entrance to the famous straits of that name. It is enough to make a man quote the spirited lines of Kipling :

"O, the blazing tropic night when the wake's a welt of light
    That holds the hot sky tame,
And the steady forefoot snores through the planet-powdered floors,
    Where the scared whale flukes in flame!"

Round the horn we fly, wrestling with giant seas, and then, while penguins and fur-seals go sporting and barking around the *Swift*, we pass the rugged, half-glaciered island of Terra del Fuego. Warmer, day by day, grows the air and softer. At last, though never a spouter have we yet raised out of the ocean, our hog-yoke tells us we are upon the rich off-shore whaling grounds.

After we had been out from home eight long months we chanced to speak the full-rig ship

William Rotch, and I then beheld a sight that
stirred my soul from truck to keelson and knocked
my youthful emotions galley-endwise. For the
Rotch had a monstrous whale, just taken, tethered
alongside.

There he lay, a bit ingloriously, to be sure, for
he was riding belly uppermost and tail foremost;
but I felt like a Titan when I looked at him.
That was the prey I had gone a-seeking. I was a
fighter of dragons and worse. Oh, what more
heroic opportunity is offered to man or boy than
to join battle with such a monster as that? So
thought I (turning sea-green the while with envy
of yonder lucky crew) and longed, with inexpres-
sible heart-hunger, for our own first whale-fight.
Moreover, I wished myself at that moment a
blood-thirsty pirate; for, ethical considerations
aside, it would have been a gratifying relief to
my feelings had we boarded that ship, like
" gentlemen of fortune," bowie-knifed her gallant
crew, and stolen that whale away.

We kept company with the *Rotch* all night, and
we "gammed" — that is to say, we exchanged
visits back and forth, and enjoyed a general
fo'c'sle pow-wow for'ard while the officers made
merry in the cabins; and particularly merry they
were that evening, too, for the old man's brother

was mate of the *William Rotch,* and the two had not come face to face for many an eventful year.

But who knoweth what a day may bring forth?

The sun came red and fierce and savage out of the water. The morning mist lifted lazily off the ocean. The long-expected happened.

Try how I will, I cannot recall in any former or any subsequent experience, whether upon land or sea, such a panic and stampede of emotions as instantly followed a ringing cry from the mast-head.

"There she blows!" I heard a man shout.

A haze seemed to rush over my soul. All that happened in the next five minutes is an utter confusion of tumultuous and ungovernable impressions. "All hands" must have been called, but I could not hear the words. Every man sprang toward his boat — in fact, the movements of the crew were automatic and inerrant — yet I made nothing coherent of their desperate hurry. Almost in an instant the boats were lowered swift away; but not until three long whale-boats were dashing out after the great leviathan and bent now upon actual chase, did I come to myself far enough to take good account of how this vast concern was being brought to pass.

I have heard of buck fever. But, lands and seas, it is nothing to whale fever!

Nevertheless, in the midst of so crazed a mood, I did, without so much as considering it, my appointed duty which, for all that, was not difficult; being, as long beforehand I had been instructed, to remain on board and do nothing. That was a simple task, but by no means agreeable.

It was certainly a vivid contradiction, as I have often since reflected, that while I, who was least in the struggle, went clean daft for the moment, the whale, who was of all concerned most gravely implicated, lay spouting contentedly only a small way from the *Swift*, and as wholly free from worry or care as a comfortable cow nibbling pink and white clover-tops.

" Boy," said the cooper, for he stood next to me and together we watched the chase, " I'll bet my go-ashore shirt and pantaloons they'll set you a-turning that 'ar grin-stun ! "

This sage observation was the expression of a splendid optimism, for when a whale is being cut in, the cabin-boy turns the grindstone while the cooper sharpens the cutting-spades.

" Oh, by Reuben Ranzo ! " yelled the cooper, grabbing me by the collar, " They'll galley him ! "

Then, tightening his grip on my neck till I thought he would strangle me, he emphasized his sudden plunge into pessimism with a blast of emphatic and unmistakable English.

Luckily for my continued existence, the fortunes of the whale-chase suddenly grew brighter. The cooper loosed his unconscious grip on my throat and leaned out over the rail, his eyes bulging with intense interest.

The chief mate's boat approached the column of steam that rose from the whale's spout-hole.

The harpooner hurled his merciless iron.

The iron took hold in the quivering flesh of the whale, and instantly the captain's boat dashed up and a second harpoon went hurtling through the air to plant itself close to the first. The whale writhed with sudden pain and fright, but did not go down. He preferred to fight.

The old man, however, had plans of his own; he would kill the whale, and that immediately.

He bellowed a hasty order to the mate, thinking to drive the mate's boat out of his way, but he had not calculated upon the stubborn ambition of that hot-headed officer. The mate never budged.

Enraged at his opposition, the captain crowded in between the mate and the monster, and ran his lance into the whale's vitals. Then there was such a commotion as I had never before witnessed. The whale went into a frantic flurry, barrels-full of

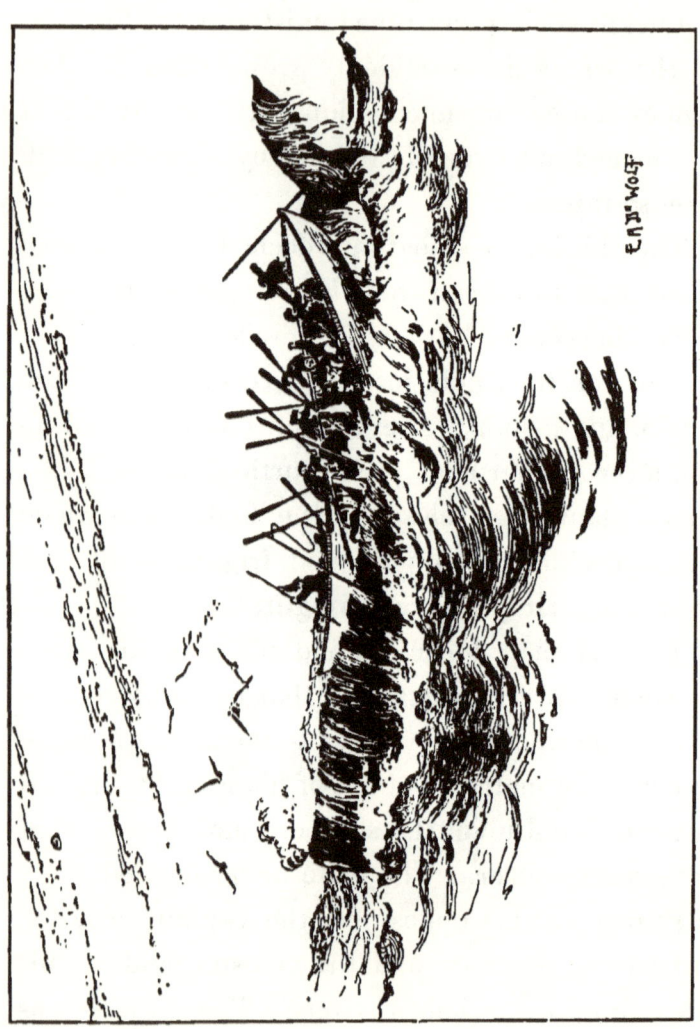

OUR FIRST SPERM WHALE.

rich, dark blood were hurled into the air from his spout-hole, the boats dashed away from him as they would from an enraged sea-serpent, and behold — a half-dozen men floundering about in the water!

"Stoven!" yelled the cooper, renewing his unconscious assaults upon my collar. "Served him dead right, I swear! An' bless ye, boy, the old lobster-back can't swim a stroke!"

Indeed he could not. There was the captain in the water, as helpless as a lady, and two of his men were trying their best to keep him from sinking, while one of the two uninjured boats was coming up to take him aboard.

"Same old yarn," said the cooper. "I've sailed with the old man five year if I've sailed a day, an' I tell ye, boy, he's done this lubberly trick forty times over. Gits wearisome, now an' then, dead wearisome for them Jacks to float a poor lubber that won't learn swimmin', and dead wearisome for poor old Chips to have to mend the old man's boat after every blessed chase."

"Then why doesn't the captain learn to swim?"

The cooper ventured no answer. He was watching the mate getting a line fast to Old Blubber. Suddenly he bethought himself of grindstone and spades, and as quickly was off to make ready for the work that would turn me into a slavish minion.

Even before the boats had come in and had got the whale alongside and well into the fluke-chains, the grinding of spades began.

Often and often I had heard men of the sea tell how a whale was cut in and tried out, but now, with my own lucky eyes, I was to see the thing done.

But before I describe how the whale was cut in, I must say something about whales in general.

There are many kinds, but only two are of importance to whalemen. The right whale is sought for his bone. The sperm whale is sought for his blubber. We of the *Swift* were sperm whaling.

Pictures of whales are uniformly deceptive. They give the impression that a good part of the animal (not fish, — a whale is a hot-blooded mammal) can be seen above the surface of the sea. They also indicate that a whale's spout is made of water. It is no such thing. All you can commonly see of a whale from the ship's deck is his spout and that is a mere column of vapor. It's his breath. Get that once in mind and you'll never call a whale a fish. You never saw a fish breathe air. You never found a fish warm enough

to belch out white vapor on a summer's day like a
steamboat.

Such, then, is the whale's spout. And by the
spout the two kinds of whales, sperm and right,
can be distinguished. A sperm whale has but one
spout-hole, and throws the spout forward at an
angle of about forty-five degrees — a thick spout
and not very high, rising from a point near the
whale's "nose." A right whale has two spout-
holes, very close together. They are about
eighteen feet from the end of his head and, of
course, much nearer his lungs than is the case
with the sperm whale. Consequently the vapor
shoots up higher and as straight as a mast. It
spreads as it rises. I suppose, too, that the big-
ness of a whale is something few landsmen could
well give account of. As a matter of fact, a sixty-
foot whale is about as big as you will ever see.
Big enough, says any whaleman — big enough to
serve as a very worthy adversary to pigmy man
who goes to slay him!

Very naturally you ask, as Brutus did (or was
it Cassius?): "What meat has this, our Cæsar
fed on, that he is grown so great?"

That depends on your whale. The sperm
whale, having teeth, lives on deep-sea jelly-fish.
The right whale, which is as toothless as any

dotard, lives on a tiny red creature called *brit,* no larger than a spider, but so numerous as to color the water a yellowish red over whole acres.

It is because of his choice of diet that the right whale has his mouth filled with a huge sieve of whalebone. That sieve is to let the *brit* through and to shut bigger sea-things out.

The arrangement is a decided success. I have seen a right whale make a scoop of his broad lips and rush through a field of *brit* (like a snow-plow through a drift) and leave a trail of blue water behind him. That is a sight to remember and also a sound to remember, for when a right whale is feeding he spouts with tremendous force. At such a time you will have no hope of striking him.

But right whales don't concern me nor do I concern right whales. We were after oil and we wanted sperm whales or none.

The oil is made from the blubber, mainly, and the blubber covers the whale like a thick coating of fat pork. In one sense it is a blanket; it keeps the whale warm in the coldest sea-water. In another sense it is a shell — or even a padded coat; it relieves the tremendous pressure of the water upon the whale's body when he sounds to the depths of the sea.

Sperm whales have, as already intimated, their ups and downs. A large sperm whale remains under water from forty-five minutes to an hour and a quarter. That is a fact to go by. When a whale has sounded and you are waiting for him to come up, it is a relief to know that some sort of limit is set upon his delay. But that is not all. You can judge where he will come up. For a whale travels, unless vigorously disturbed, about two miles an hour. So you note which way he headed when he sounded, and you measure off two miles in that direction, and you know where to meet your friend again. This is an infallible rule whenever it works.

But a whale has something beside ups and downs and blubber. He has a marvellous sagacity. By some mysterious process, which I suppose the Society for Psychical Research would call "thought transference," whales pass the news of disaster from one end of a school to another. When one of the company is wounded, every whale within a radius of four miles is advised of the fact. Sometimes the alarm will bring speedy assistance. That gives the whaleman only a better chance to ply his gainful trade. Sometimes a retreat is ordered. The whole squadron will dash away as by some instantaneous common impulse, evidently terror-struck.

Can a sperm whale be called a globe-trotter? Be that as it may, the sperm whale migrates far and wide. Ships cruise on the shores of Chili and Peru at a distance of from two to one hundred leagues from the shore, and you will often see both in- and off-shore vessels doing nothing. At other times all will be engaged. Where were the whales while the ships lay idle? Roving over the broad seas, no doubt, and many a mile away, a-taking of their ease.

It is known to a solid certainty that whales have been harpooned in the Atlantic ocean, and have been afterward taken in the Pacific. The marks on the irons proved the identity of the whale every time. Old Blubber seems to travel for change of scene. It is clear that he is not led to migrate by any fear of the whalemen. Indeed, whales are not easily driven away from their feeding-ground by ships.

But whatever the ups and downs of that whale alongside the *Swift,* and whatever the vicissitudes of his travelling days, one thing was clear. That whale was dead. Like Marley of blessed memory, he was dead as a door-nail. Unlike Marley, however, he could never come to life again. They were cutting him in. I saw it done.

I beheld two stages slung over the side of the ship, each stage six feet long and a foot wide. Men stood upon the stages with sharp spades — one to cut the blubber, the other to kill the sharks that would have devoured our prize.

I saw an aperture made near the whale's fin. I saw the great hook inserted. I saw a semi-circle cut around the hook.

Then they took the falls to the windlass. The windlass wound in the chain. The chain passed through a block at the main-mast head. The chain then became the tackle, heaved hard at the iron hook, and stripped the blubber from the whale.

The blubber came off in a continuous spiral strip. The whale meanwhile kept turning over and over in the water. The ripping of the blubber from the carcass was guided by the sharp spade of the officer on the stage.

I saw a strip of white, pork-like blubber, twenty-five feet long and five feet wide, hoisted into a perpendicular position and its top touching the mast-head. Then they cut the piece ("blanket-piece," they said) loose from the whale and lowered the blubber into the ship's hold between decks, at the same time attaching the other tackle to a fresh cut in the whale's flesh and preparing to raise another blanket-piece.

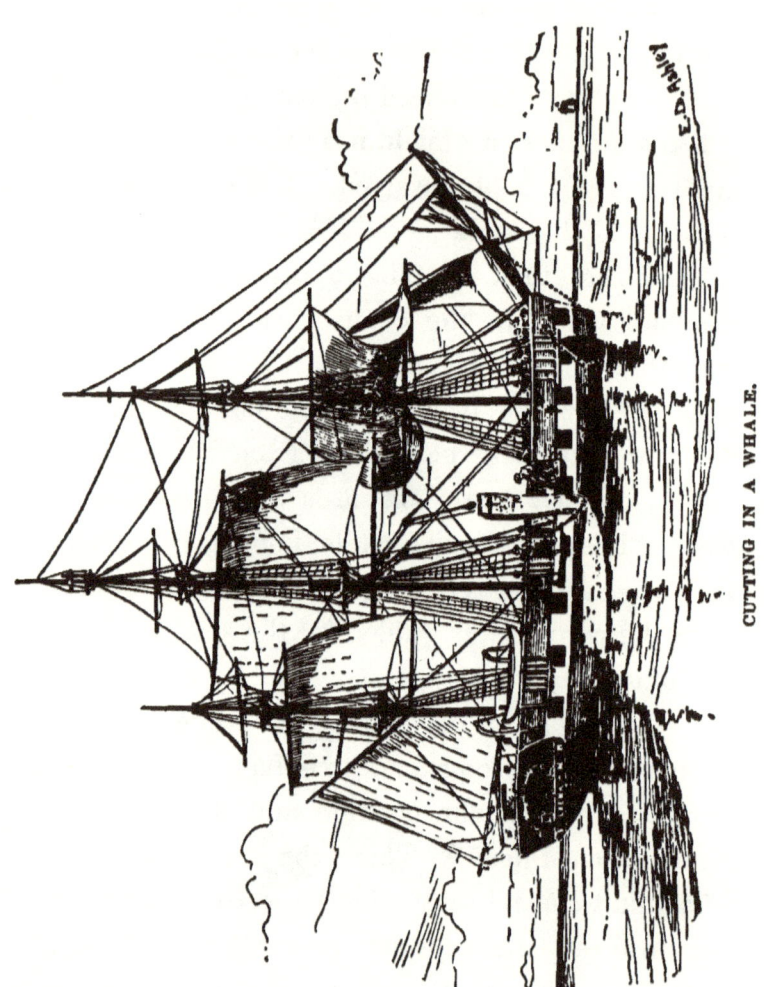

CUTTING IN A WHALE.

I saw this process repeated until the blubber was stripped from the whale.

I saw the head cut off from the huge beast and hoisted on deck. I felt the great ship strain. The standing-rigging on the starboard side slackened. The mast bent over like a whip-stock. I saw the *Swift* listed till her plank-shear was nearly level with the water.

A filthy column of black smoke rose out of the try-works. They were cutting the blubber into horse-pieces, mincing these pieces, and putting the hashed blubber into huge pots with brick flooring under them and a blazing fire of blubber scraps blazing around them. Thence the oil passed into a huge copper cooler and thence in turn into casks.

They made merry over the boiling. They nibbled bits of fried blubber, and they fried doughnuts in the grease.

The whole ship was befouled, but we soon had her cleaned up again, man-o'-war fashion; and what was better yet, we coopered a hundred barrels of oil.

"Lands and seas," said I to myself, "this is the biggest business afloat or ashore."

But as yet I had not chased a whale.

BRINGING MR. TOWNSEND
BACK AGAIN.

" Escape me ?
Never.
Beloved! "
—Browning.

" Tell me, messmate, why in the name of all that's shipshape did *you* ever come to sea ? "

" Shiver my soul if I can tell ! "

" *I'll* tell you, boy, *I'll* tell you. You come to sea just to see the world. Ain't I right, Jack ? All you come for was just to see the world. You wanted to clap your blinkin' top-lights on Nuka-hiva, an' Upolo, an' Hivaoa, an' the Cape, an' Mahee, an' all them high-saoundin' places you hearn tell on when you was knee-high to a marlin' spike."

The older man spoke with an air of preternatural knowingness. He leaned forward insinuatingly upon the stout iron hoop that ran under his arms. The youth, as he listened to this relentless diagnosis of his distemper, lolled back upon his own iron hoop and thrust his half-akimbo elbows out across it. The two whalemen were upon lookout duty at the mainmast head of that staunch old hooker, the whaling ship *Swift.*

"Taownsend," the old sea-dog continued, " I don't much blame you for coming, but by the bloody wars you're a fool if you desert. We've had blasted poor luck, I know, blasted poor. And I know, too, we've all got to lose by it, every Jack Tar of us, all the way from the old man on the quarter-deck down to Charlie Robbins in the cabin. Some ways I'd rather be to sea in a merchantman and git reg'lar wages 'stid o' goin' by lays. But I tell you, Taownsend, you're a blarsted ninny if you try to get aout o' this butter-box. First place, them tattoo natives'll make dunder-funk o' your tender timbers 'fore you been ashore half a day. Nex' place, you'll never git a lift off that there island if you once git on it — you'll just be a low-daown beach comber all the rest o' your natchral days. Third place, the old man'll git the darbies on you 'n less 'n a week an' then you'll be back aboard o' here an' wishin' you was plumb dead."

A very determined look glaring out of the old blubber hunter's sharp eyes showed that he thought his logic invincible.

One fact, however, he had wholly overlooked. Townsend was in debt to the old man. He had shipped for a long lay and had a thumping big bill for outfitting and board before we sailed from

old New Bedford. So if he remained in the *Swift*
throughout the voyage he would have little or
nothing coming to him at its conclusion. Therefore, from Townsend's standpoint it was worth
while to take big risks and try to ship again.
The venture involved no loss and a possible gain.

So, despite the grave counsel from the ancient
mariner, this daring young citizen of Rochester,
N. Y., gazed wistfully toward the splendid wooded
island — one of the Navigator group, better known
under the name of Samoa — which rose majesti-
cally out of the ocean, green, luxuriant, fascinating.
It was scarce two miles away.

"My stars!" said Townsend to himself, "my
stars, if I was only there!"

No amount of good advice could change Townsend's determination to leave the ship. Old
Bowline might have informed the officers of Townsend's plans, but he thought he had talked the
boy out of his folly. So the project developed
quite as if it had suffered nothing by interference.

We cruised so near the Samoa Islands that not
infrequently the natives would come off in canoes,
bringing the usual commodities — fruit, cocoanuts,
fowl and pigs — to trade for cotton cloth, gunpowder, iron hoops, and the trinkets and gimcracks
they always find so desirable.

It often happened that a canoe would bring along as trader and interpreter some renegade whaleman who had deserted his ship and turned " beachcomber," living among the natives, and little better than the worst of them. This is one of the strangest things about sailoring. A seaman's civilization will drop off like the cast skin of a rattlesnake when he goes to live among savages.

While trading was going on — and it would sometimes last two days at a stretch — the old man would keep one of the brown-skinned, yellow-haired, frizzle-headed tatooed natives on board as a hostage. The old man had learned caution by bitter experience. At Hivaoa we had found it by no means easy to keep the natives from kidnapping a red-haired sailor. They thought his scalp worth more than his life. At Auhuga one of our men was actually roasted and eaten.

That was a lesson to remember. We never took chances after that. But with a native hostage on board the ship, we were not afraid to go a long way in-shore in our boats, though we never quite ventured to land. When the trading was done and we were about to leave, we would send the hostage off in one of our boats, and as soon as we came within swimming distance of the shore we would pitch him overboard and make him paddle for *terra firma*.

Now it was on one of these occasions, when a hostage was being returned to the bosom of his tribe, that the Rochester boy found an opportunity to desert. He was in the boat as we took off the native, and when the tatooed man was about to start ashore, Townsend suddenly jumped overboard and swam for the land. The officer in charge ordered him to return, but he never paid the least attention — just tumbled through the surf, scrambled up the beach and made away inland as fast as his truant heels could carry him.

"Blast my luck," said the officer, "blast my ugly luck! *Now* I'll have to face the music! *Now* the old man'll make me waltz!" But he checked the outpouring of his chagrined rage. He tried to recover something like dignity before his men. The men, on their part, suppressed their merriment. Without another word from anybody the boat returned to the ship.

It was just as the second mate had predicted. The old man flew into a terrible passion, swore hideous blasts of blubber-slicer profanity, cursed everybody and everything from the chief mate to the carpenter's ditty-box, and vowed *he'd* have that Townsend back in his clutches again if he had

to chase him till the end of time. *He* didn't care
what it cost. *He'd* get even with that cussed
young beach-comber if he had to die for it, and
all the rest of us along with him. He'd rather
get a good fierce grip on Ed. Townsend than try
out the last sperm whale in the South Pacific —
he'd be *blowed* if he wouldn't!

But, as on former occasions, we saw the gale
blow by. The worse the old man raged the
sooner he would calm down. And when the
tempest was over, all that remained of the case
against Townsend was a sincere desire, with
a proportionate determination, to recover the
services of so good a sailor.

So the next day we stood in to another bay,
about four miles to the leeward of the place that
had witnessed Townsend's escape. There, unable
to drop our mud-hook, we lay off and on.

We had not been long in the bay before a canoe
came off with a white man and two natives. That
was just the very thing the old man wanted. He
received the visitors with eager welcome, invited
them into the cabin, ordered drinks for four, and
dismissed the steward, warning him to shut the
door tight behind him.

The quartette remained in solemn executive
session for half an hour. Then the cabin door

opened, the men came up on deck, and as the visitors clambered down into their canoe again I heard the old man whisper over the rail, "Now remember, my man, *two white flags* and you get your reward!"

Then we stood off and put to sea, cruising the grounds again looking for whales.

One warm, bright, clear-shining Southern morning we were fanning along under a cloud of canvas over a delightfully smooth sea, when a cry from the clouds called down the spirited warning I had heard on a former occasion :

"There she blows!   Sperm whale!"

"Where away?"

There was breathless excitement on deck.   My heart hammered against my ribs.   I shook with bewildered suspense.

"Four points on the lee bow, sir."

The words stabbed through and through me.

"How far off?"

"Three miles, sir."

The captain was in his element.   His eyes blazed.   His face was white.   His voice was harsh and strident.   He was master of a splendid occasion.

"Call all hands!" he thundered.   "Get your boats ready!   Square the mainyard!   Put the helm up and keep her off!" Heavens, what confusion!

"Stand by your boats!"

At that, every man knew his place and sprang for it with an eager bound of joy. I was among them. For the first time in my young life I was to go in a whale-boat. I was in the mate's boat.

"Lower away boats!" bellowed His Majesty.

Instantly the mate and the boat-steerer sprang into the cedar boat — one in either end, boat-steerer forward, officer aft — and our crew were over the ship's side before the boat splashed in the water. We pounced upon our thwarts, seized our long oars, looked sharp astern, and took the prompt word of command. I pulled after oar.

The sail was up in a twinkling. It bellied out full. We dashed headlong after our prey. We were in the lead. The captain and the second mate followed close.

I shall never forget the dazzling sensations of that first moment — the tall ship, with her checkered sides and her huge white davits; the two sharp-bowed clinker built boats — five long oars in each; two on one side, three on the other; the sun-glint upon the oar-blades as they lifted above the surface, the white splash when they dipped again; the rapid, nervous, brutal stroke;

the pose of the officers as they stood in the stern-
sheets of the boats, each with his lifted left hand
holding the steering oar, and each with his right
hand pushing upon the stroke oar ; and, yet more
vivid, the one figure I could see in our own boat.
For the mate stood last, steering with one hand
and helping me row with the other.

How those men sprang to their oars — it makes
my blood tingle to recall. The oars bent in the
water. We ripped through the waves, the spray
dashing high and white. We were chasing the
whale !

And here is the wonderful thing. I had not yet
got a glimpse of the whale. In the confusion and
excitement of lowering away, I had not even seen
the column of vapor that marked him to view. I
sat toiling in that pitching and careening boat,
with my back toward the whale.

It was terrible — going to my death, it might
be, and going backward !

The mate's face reassured me. He was cool
and determined — teeth clenched, eyes glaring,
brows knitted, but not a sign of anxiety. He
knew no such thing as fear.

He thrust out his chin. I could see the cords
draw stiff in his neck. His face was red from
exertion. Every nerve thrilled with a fierce joy.

He whispered encouragement to his crew — hissed it — gasped it.

"Spring hard, my lively hearties! Spring hard! Break a stick, will you? will you? break a stick! Come, come, come, — spring *hard!*"

We pulled like mad.

"Not a word — not a word! If you make the least bit of noise I'll brain every one of you! Come, come, — break an oar!"

We exerted ourselves to the uttermost. We bent the oars till I thought they would snap in two.

"Give away, boys! Spring hard!"

The captain tried his best to outfoot us. The water leaped in foam around the prow of his boat. Suddenly the mate's face changed. He bit his lip. His eyes stared fixedly. He threw back his head.

"Peak your oar," he hissed. Then he shouted, "Stand up and *let him have it!*"

I thought my heart would burst. Everything swam before me. I gripped my oar tight. I thought I was fainting.

"Starn all," the mate roared. "Starn all, and get out of the suds!"

I fell forward with my full weight upon my oar. The mast and sail came down as by magic. The mate rushed forward; the harpooner rushed aft; they changed places. The line leaped out of its Flemish coil in the tub.

We were fast to a whale!

The whale sounded and the line flew after him. It smoked around the loggerhead, it buzzed as it raced past the men, it groaned in the chocks. They poured water on the loggerhead to keep it from taking fire. The whale, with two harpoons in him, took two hundred fathoms of our line.

He was gone but five minutes.

Then, oh the horror! A vast, black, shining mass stood up ten feet out of water on our lee beam. It was the whale. He had come up head first, a hundred feet away.

The boat-steerer swung the steering-oar with all his might. The boat instantly turned half about.

"Haul line, all hands!" whispered the boat-steerer. The Manila line came in wet and heavy, and ran back into the stern-sheets. We were gaining upon our prey.

"Take your oars now."

Again we were brought with our backs to the whale. The awful moment was at hand. Oh, for eyes in the back of my head! The officer must already be standing up, lance in hand, ready to strike the murderous blow.

The boat-steerer's mouth was half-open with expectancy — and behold! Almost against our boat, and just awash of the surface, the monstrous black bulk of the whale! He stretched huge and dim under water. Only part of him could be seen. A slanting column of hot white vapor stood up ten feet tall, like a rakish mast. It was the whale's spout.

When the mate's lance had been sent into the whale's vitals, the boat dashed away from the monster, and I got my first good view of him. He was cutting and thrashing like a cat in a fit. The water all round him was crimson. Jets of thick, cloggy blood — a hogsheadful at each jet — leaped six feet high from his spout-hole. Then gradually the jets grew feebler. Then the blood merely poured out. Then the whale took a swift, wide circle against the sun, threw his whole mass out of water, breaching; fell on his side with a hideous, wallowing splash; stuck one fin up, quivering; dropped his huge, ivory-toothed jaw, and lay dead, in a lather of blood and foam!

An involuntary yell of triumph went up simultaneously from all three boats.

We rowed up to the whale, and before we attached our tow-rope, the mate ran his lance into the whale's eye to make sure the life was all gone

out of him. He never even quivered. So the
line was made fast to a slit cut in old Blubber's
spout-hole, and we towed his huge carcass to the
Swift. On the way thither, Brother Bowline,
who was pulling bow oar, leaned forward between
strokes, and said, in jerky phrases interrupted by
his work, " I tell you, Charlie, young Townsend
would be sorry enough — if he could see us now,
don't you — say so, boy? Never saw prettier
fight, no — body hurt, nothin' broke. Lord, how
I pity that fool on the island ! "

It amazed me to see how easily we towed the
tremendous, sixty-foot carcass. After we once
got the whale started he seemed to propel himself.
You would never think it from his " model," and
yet the big beast can run like a race-horse when
he's alive. The motion is all but effortless — a
little squirming movement of the tail sends him
whizzing through the water.

We cut that whale in and boiled out his blubber.

Then we set about a most unaccountable task.
The old man ordered it and we had to obey, but
we growled while we worked. The task was no
less than the sending down of our light yards —
top-gallants and royals — and the striking of fore
and mizzen-top-gallant masts. There seemed to
be no need for such a procedure. There was only

a very light breeze blowing, and not a sign of a storm anywhere.

Old Bowline thought the crew were being hazed. He reminded his shipmates that the old man had had "such times" before. Didn't every man remember pounding the anchor hour after hour? Could anybody forget the unnecessary holystoning of the deck? Had nobody any recollection of wearing out his knees pushing a "prayer book" — and swearing inside his jumpers while he did it?

I, for my part, had quite different suspicions. I could not shake myself wholly free of the notion that all this change aboard the *Swift* was in some way connected with the old man's farewell admonition to the beach-comber: "Remember, now, *two white flags*, and you get your reward!"

After ten days had gone by, an island rose proudly out of the ocean.

It was the same green, wooded paradise we had last put out from — a beautiful, mountainous oasis, if one may so speak, in the vast waste of blue waters.

We stood in for the beach-comber's bay, my fancy big with expectancy. I knew now why the old man had disguised the ship.

It all fell out just as I had expected. We beat our way up the harbor, and I watched the shore with eager eyes. Presently I saw a canoe coming off, dancing on the swell, her paddles dipped first one side and then the other, six Kanakas on her thwarts and a white man in either end. Each white man held up a white flag.

Full of waggish fun, the old man made ready to wear ship as soon as the canoe approached, and when the *Swift* came round so as to expose the five bold capitals painted across her stern, one of the white flags went down as if the man in the canoe's prow had suddenly been shot. The man fell flat in the bottom of the canoe, burying his face in his hands.

He was our man Townsend!

The beach-comber brought the canoe alongside, and her crew, Townsend not excepted, clambered on board.

We shouted with wicked glee. " What'd I tell you," said Old Bowline. " Didn't I tell you you was a blarsted ninny ever to desert ? Now you've got your come-up-ance ! " I called out, " Hoist by your own petard ; hanged on your own gallows; caught by your own flag ! " But the captain called us all aft and prepared to lay down the law.

We stood in a sort of loose ring on the quarter-deck. Townsend faced the captain. Poor truant, he was pale as the ship's courses !

The old man looked the picture and personification of awful wrath.

"Townsend," he began in a sepulchral tone that made us all shiver — but he never got any further with his intended oration.

"Ha! ha! ha-a-a!" he bellowed. "Thought you'd run away from the captain of the whaling ship *Swift*, *didn't you?* Oh, ha! — ha! — ha! — ha-a-a! Come, my hearties, just tow this deserter before the mast and tell him what you think of him! Far as I'm concerned I've got only this to say: if the poor fool plays me another trick like this, *I'll* make it *hot* for him!"

Then, turning to the beach-comber, he said, "We'll settle accounts in the cabin, if you like!"

RIGHT WHALES.

We cruised about three months in the Southern Ocean, looking for right whales. We saw many, and took six hundred barrels of oil and about five thousand pounds of bone.

One day, when the weather was fine and the ocean very calm, we lowered and gave chase to two monstrous right whales that were going slowly to the leeward. The captain's boat came up to them first, and succeeded in striking one.

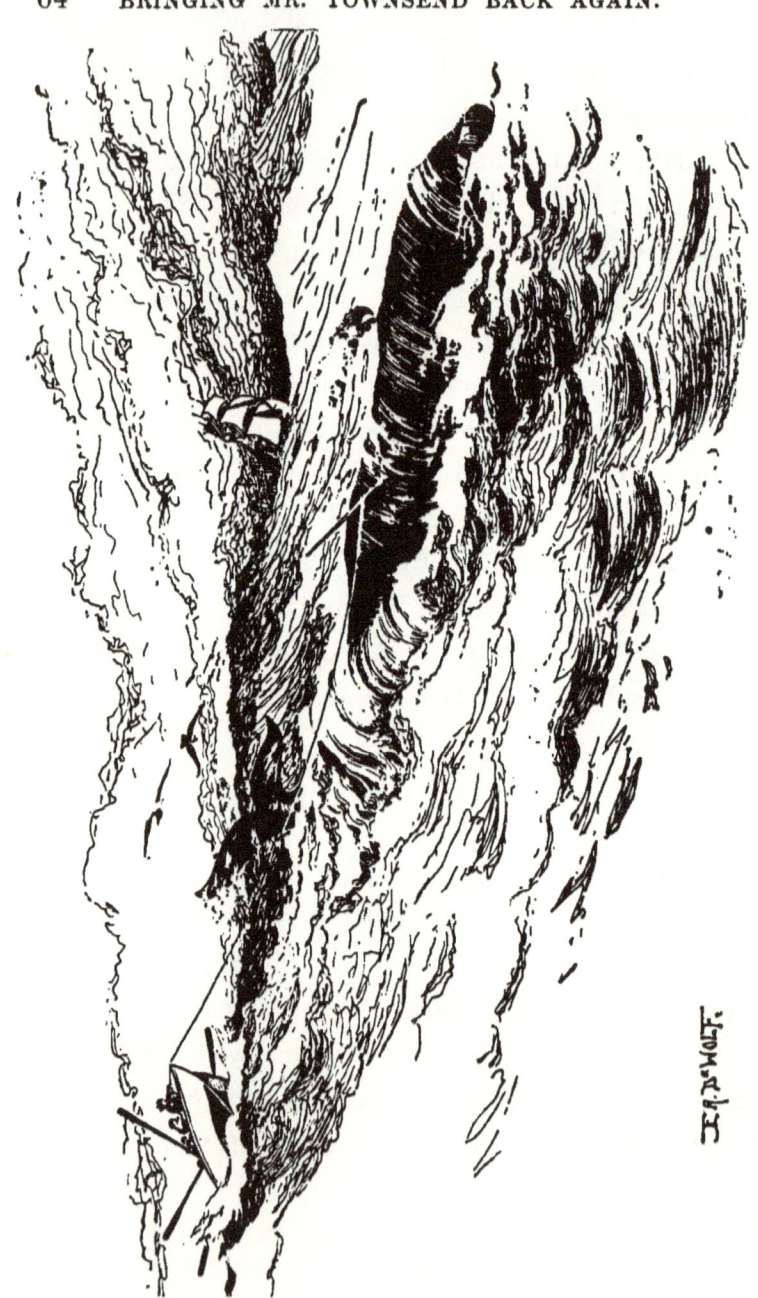

OUR FIRST RIGHT WHALE.

Instantly down went both the whales. When they came up again, the mate struck the other one. They proved to be a bull and a cow — the cow was struck first.

The bull made the sea foam. He cut around in great fury and stove two of our boats — the captain's and the mate's — and the lines had to be cut to get clear. The second mate came along lively and picked up the crews, which came near sinking his boat. Eighteen men in one boat, and the ship four miles away to leeward — a pleasant prospect! And as the wind had died down completely there was nothing for it but to row, and that in an all but sinking boat, so crowded you could hardly move without knocking your neighbor overboard!

But that was not the worst of it. The worst of it fell upon myself and another dare-devil young chap — or rather he and I brought it down upon ourselves, for we volunteered. It was this way. The captain was bound not to lose sight of the stoven boats, and wanted two of the men to stay by them until he could bring the old hooker and pick them up. We two, being young and fearless, offered to take the job. We stood each on the stern and bow of a boat, sunken just to the water's edge, and hung on to a flag-pole for three

5

THE STOVEN BOATS.

terrible hours, with the two wounded whales cutting about and making the water white with their huge flukes, only a little way from where we stood.

All that while we were afraid for our lives, as we were out in the middle of the ocean and the ship was four miles off.

It is always with a shudder that I recall that adventure, though fifty years and more have gone by since then. But I remember that even when the danger was worst, we found room for joking and one of our men cried out, " Better have paid your washwoman!" That is the usual gibe when a man is caught in a stoven boat, for there is a belief among whalers that if you don't pay your washwoman you'll suffer the penalty of getting your boat smashed.

PITCAIRN'S ISLAND.

Here I insert a piece of literature penned by the *Swift's* mate and contributed to Ellis's " History of New Bedford."

" Making our passage to the eastward," says he, " when in the longitude of Pitcairn's Island, the ship was put to the north, and at 8 A. M. on the next day, we made the land, appearing more like a sail or ship in the long distance. On nearing we found the island to be nearly 2000 feet high, and about five miles in circumference, with a ledge of rocks making off a few rods from the north and south points. When within two miles of the islands five of the natives came off in their canoes, the canoes being dug out of a tree ten or twelve feet long and about two feet wide, with keel from three to four inches broad.

" The natives, before coming on board, very politely asked permission of the captain. They speak very good English when talking to English or Americans, but not intelligibly at all to me when talking to each other, owing to their talking so very quickly. At 9 in the morning I went on shore and found it very tiresome in walking up the long, steep hill or cliff. Their houses are built of boards, planed the sides and ends. The sides ship and unship on account of its being very warm. The roofs are thatched with the leaves of the trees. We found the people very friendly and hospitable; the young married and single women very diffident. They are tall — the most of them — and handsomely shaped. Their every-day dress is a loose gown, with no shoes, bonnet, or handkerchief. The children are very pretty and healthy and are good scholars. The

THE SHIP "SWIFT" OFF PITCAIRN'S ISLAND.

boys at ten and eleven had gone as far as the
rule of three. The men are well made, tall, with
good features, and are very strong. They are very
fair and honest in all their dealings. Their prin-
cipal industry is in cultivating the ground. The
island is equally divided among all the people. In
trading with ships every family sells an equal
share. The women are very strong. I met
several coming from the mountain. When down
to the village I took the load from some of their
backs, and counted five large watermelons as one
load. 'These women are between the ages of
thirty and forty, and the mothers of ten or twelve
children. An American lady can hardly come up
to that. The girls are marriageable at the age of
twelve, and mothers of fine children at thirteen.
Rather too young for our folks.' The above in
quotation marks is a copy from my journal, written in the fall of 1839, at the time of our visit to
the island. When the boats returned to the ship
with the captain, he was accompanied by John
Adams, the son of John Adams, one of the
survivors of the *Bounty*, the son of Lietcunant
Christian, the leader of the mutiny. By invitation of Adams I spent the night at his home.
His family consisted at this time of wife and one
daughter, and I received the most hospitable

treatment in their simple and womanly manner.
The boats coming in in the morning were loaded
with the products of the island when I returned to
the ship."

RUDDER SIMPSON, MYSELF AND THE PERSONAGE.

"Strangers in strange places should always be strangers."
— *Ruth Ashmore.*

"'TAINT much like a New Bedford Sunday, eh boy?"

"Not by a long sea mile!"

"Church in the morning — Holy Joe in his heavenly togs. Bull-fight in the afternoon — Holy Joe on deck with blood in his for'ard lights, b'gawsh! *Granny Howland!* what a crew these here heathen Chilenos be! Eh, boy?"

"Pious, though."

"Eh?"

"Pious, Rudder, pious as a saint in a stained-glass window. I was on shore yesterday; and Rudder, you ought to've seen the turn-out. Beats man-o'-war's men at quarters. Pretty as a New Bedford Fourth-o'-July. Long strings o' priests and such; big crew o' sogers; band o' music; flags and candles; and all the dagoes in Talcahuano turned loose and shouting Spanish so I thought they'd bust an oar — sure! I gave

chase, o' course, and they made off to windward
and brought up in some kind o' big square."

"*Plaza*," said Rudder.   "That's what these
here heathen Chilienos calls it."

"Yes," I went on, "that's the word.   Funny
lingo they talk here.   And, Rudder, that whole
turn-out was brought up all standing by an order
from the colonel, or general, or whatever they
call their ' old man,' and then they got out a
dummy of Judas Iscariot."

" Effigy," laughed Rudder, " That's the word
you're soundin' for."

" Well, *effigy* then.   That whole ship's company
fell in line again, and peppered that effigy with
cold lead.   Then they set the old moss-back afire,
beginning with his boots. and when the fire crept
up amidships he blew himself to bits, like a bomb
lance. and all the people yelled and jumped and
crowed.   Don't you call *that* pious, Rudder ?"

" Well, t'ain't my notion of piosity.   Piosity,
boy, is to keep out o' jail, keep out o' bull-fights,
and steer clear o' them dev'lish *pulparees*.   That's
what *I* call piosity.   An' them pulparees— I tell
you, boy — them pulparees is the sartin road to
Granny Howlan' 's washtub.   Why, there's one
now, boy."   (A moment of hesitation, a wriggle
of futile resistance.)   " Say we go in?"

I laughed outright. So did Rudder, and in we went.

A pulparee is by interpretation a grog-shop. *Pulparia* is the Spanish, but we mariners give it a turn of our own. Dark and grimy is the pulparee; desperate and dangerous are the idlers that lounge there ; vile and strong is the fiery liquor they drink.

I stepped across the well-worn threshold with a stinging sense of guilt. I had never entered such a place before. I was a thorough-going tecto-taller. And besides I began to wonder how ever should I manage to comport myself becomingly in the fellowship of these hard and reckless chole drinkers. I was sorry, now, that I had let Rudder Simpson take me in tow.

My embarrassment, however, was soon relieved, for a superb native, gorgeous in many dazzling colors, stepped up to Simpson and engaged him in conversation.

" Bowling-alleyo," said the glittering stranger, " Señor lika play nine-pinza ? "

" You're right," said Rudder, flattered with the attention, " Where away ? "

" Come," said the dazzling personage, with a stagy gesture. He looked as if he had just stepped out of " Carmen."

The Personage led the way into the street, and we followed. We passed on together along a thoroughfare crowded with Chilian merrymakers. Here an organ grinder had gathered a motley crowd of listeners. Yonder a man and a woman, both *peones*, were dancing the *zamacueca*. Leisurely throngs strolled by on their way to the bull-fight. Now and then a pretty *señorita* peered out at us through a grated window piercing some stout adobe wall.

Spanish was spoken on every hand. Rudder and I enjoyed the novelty of the situation. It was a great thing to have a notable personage to serve as guide and guardian, as we roamed through that old, white-walled, red-tiled Chilian town.

We came at last to a sort of cheap inn, or *posada*, entering which, we crossed the enclosed *patio* and found ourselves in the bowling alley.

Here the Personage bargained with the sallow, round-shouldered, little proprietor, and explained to Rudder the terms of the agreement. It was simplicity itself. The loser of the game was to pay for the use of the alley.

Then the game began. The Personage threw off his emerald-hued *poncho* and gave it to me to hold.

With a magnificent wave of his patrician hand, he said to me, " You, señor, pick up ze nine-pinza!"

Rudder could not have made me do it. I should have fought to the last eyelash. But for the personage — why, *certainly, with pleasure!*

It was a great treat to watch those two men play. What a curious contrast! The Personage would take his *cigarrito* between the fingers of his left hand, poise the wooden ball in the palm of his right hand, strike a startling, statuesque attitude, and then, with a sudden spring that sent the long red sash swinging against his yellow breeches, and brought the huge silver spurs of his tall boots banging against the floor, he would hurl the ball down the alley. Then he would pose like Hamlet when he says, " To be or not to be," and wait to see the result.

Rudder, on the other hand, rolled into range with a slovenly waddle and discharged his missile without further ado. *Whish-sh-sh-sht, bumpety-bump-bump-bump, whir-r-r-r, crash!* Down would go the nine-pins — never less than six — generally all nine! But with the Personage it was not so. Had he been drinking *augadente* — who knows?

I picked up nine-pins for fully an hour. From time to time I saw a pained look in the Personage's proud face, for the Personage was playing a losing game.

When the hour was done, Rudder said, " Now colonel, you settle with the Czar ! "

" *I* — how you saya? *I* paya ze gamo? No, señor, *no !* You win, you paya ! I lose ze gamo. You lose ze *oro* — how you saya ? — ze monee ! "

" No, ye don't," cried Rudder. " Blowed if ye do ! "

" Si, señor. How you say ? — *yes, sirra !* "

" Blast ye ?" bawled Rudder. " Pay down that cash or I'll make old rags out o' yer rainbow togs. *Blowed* if I don't ! Hear that, *Dago ?*"

Now, as a matter of solemn fact, the Personage had not so much as a piastre in his wallet. He had already spent his last copper for *augadente* in the pulparce.

Rudder was not uncommonly quick of perception. It was a moment before he fully grasped the enormity of the outrage the Personage had perpetrated upon him. When he saw through the scheme, he boiled with wrath. Before he had time to lay into the Personage, the round-shouldered proprietor stuck his sallow visage through the door of his lair, and seeing what was up, made haste to insure himself against fraud.

He expostulated fiercely with Rudder and the Personage, demanding four times the usual fee.

"Say, old hoss," said Rudder, "this sunset dandy here won't pay down the cash; an' if he don't, I'll shiver his blarsted timbers, b'gawsh! Hear *that*, ye blasted *Dago?*"

The Personage puffed his *cigarrito* in silence.

Rudder gazed at his enemy a second in unutterable malice. Then he swung his huge palm in air and brought it across the face of the Personage with a slam that knocked that worthy's *cigarritto* clean into his mouth, light and all!

Now, I flatter myself that my wits work quicker than Rudder Simpson's. In an instant I got three different views of the situation. First, this was a den of robbers and the Personage was a decoy to lead us into peril, the provocation being raised by him to induce us to begin the fight and take the consequence if ever the case got into court. Second, this was a first-class hotel, but full of the friends of the Personage, who would be willing to take his part in a quarrel. Third, the hotel was well-nigh deserted because of the bull-fight, and therefore there would be few witnesses of what might presently occur. In any contingency, the scene of the battle must be immediately transferred to the open street.

To this end I grabbed the Chileno's green *poncho*, slapped him on the head with it, to attract his attention, and then turned and ran like a gallied whale.

The Personage dashed after me, Rudder Simpson dashed after the Personage, and the round-shouldered alley-owner dashed after Rudder Simpson. I led my excited followers a swift chase across the *patio*, plunged headlong through the *posado* and brought up in the street. Once there I dropped the *poncho*, and just as I did so, the agile Simpson landed a merciless right-swing on the Chileno's starboard ear.

Neither the stoop-shouldered proprietor nor the eighteen-year-old cabin-boy cared to get mixed up in the row, so we two stood well back from the mill. We were not alone, however, for the battle was no more than joined when up came a dozen sailors from various ships in the harbor.

"I sy," bawled a ruddy Cockney, "'ere's a bloody row the syme as a bloody bull-fight! W'at's on?"

"'It 'im, Yank, 'it 'im bloomin' 'ard!"

"Avast!" cried a Nantucket whaleman. "His chimney's afire! He's spoutin' blood! It's his flurry!"

"No, 'taint; he's only a little groggy. There, my hearties, bring the claret — give away, boys!"

"That's right, Jack, you're a good 'un, 'eart an' 'and!"

"Watch 'im, *watch* 'im! *There, good* un!"

By this time the Personage had lost his silk sash, his shirt was torn open from shoulder to belt, and his hairless head was, as Dr. Doyle would say, a study in scarlet. Rudder, on the other hand, was still in prime condition. He was badly out of wind and he had a lump under his left eye like a pigeon's egg, but there was unlimited fight in that huge, lanky frame of his. He made a furious lead at his foe. The two men grappled and clinched. The Spaniard was forced to the wall.

"*Give* it to him, Yank!"

"Look sharp, Yank; 'e'll spur."

And spur he did. That was what he had been waiting for. He jabbed the sharp steel rowel deep into the calf of Rudder Simpson's leg and ground it to and fro in the wound.

"Down killick!"

"*Kill* the Dago!"

In Rudder's effort to escape the spur he had lost his balance, and the two desperate men fell to the earth together.

"Bully for you!"

"Kill 'im, Yank!"

"Don't get gallied!"

But best he could do, Rudder was forced under.

Then I heard a half-smothered cry : " Help —
quick — *more beef !* " The Spaniard was biting
Rudder Simpson's nose ! !

I sprang to the rescue. As I did so, a dozen
Chilenos came up out of the ground. A dozen
more dropped down from the sky. I battered the
Spaniard with both fists till I thought I had killed
him, and then —

Two seconds later it was several hours afterward.

I opened my eyes — or rather, my eye, for one
of them somehow stayed shut — and observed
important changes in my surroundings. Four
walls had closed around me. A low couch had
worked its way in under my back. A heavy-
raftered roof unaccountably met my gaze. In
other words, I had been carried into a house and
rescued from the blood-thirsty Chilenos.

It was night.

I took in the situation only by degrees. A dark-
eyed woman was sitting at the foot of the couch.
She was brightly clad, and she had a brilliant
shawl thrown over her shoulders. Her hair hung
in two heavy, dark braids. The woman gazed
across the room. Her attention was fixed upon
someone speaking. That someone knelt before

6

an image of the blessed Virgin, and was praying aloud to the holy Mother of God?

I had never heard such pathos in a woman's voice. It was the agony of unanswered prayer.

It was a sweet voice. The woman was very young.

I could not understand what she said, but I know she was entreating the Maid of Galilee to spare my life. I could not bear to see the woman so sad; so I moved gently on the couch.

"Oh, Inez!" cried the mother.

The girl sprang from her knees. The two women embraced each other and bent over me. Their brown eyes shown with exultant joy; their hair brushed my face.

I felt like a person suddenly required to make a speech. I had been *saved* — saved from the fury of a blood-thirsty mob; these women had saved me — I owed my life to them! Oh, how could I thank them enough? I tried to frame some sort of expression for my gratitude; but then it occurred to me that I had a capital excuse for saying absolutely nothing at all. I knew not a single word of Spanish.

What an agreeable relief!

But had I attempted even the feeblest sentence, it would inevitably have been interrupted, for just

then there was a deafening uproar in the street.
I could hear loud cries. The words were Spanish.
I could nevertheless understand one word, *Americano*, and I realized that I was the person so
earnestly held in request.

Inez rushed to the windows to make sure that
the shutters were securely barred. As she did so,
she left a pretty picture in my memory — her
white arms outstretched, her head thrown back,
her hair luxuriant and beautiful. She was my
guardian angel.

I lifted my head to watch her, but the effort
made me dizzy, and I swooned again.

I think it must have been only a few minutes
before I was myself once more, but when I next
realized the possible gravity of the situation, the
mob had gone and we were for the moment safe.
Inez sat by my side, stroking my hand and looking distractingly lovely. I noticed the pungent
odor of some foreign drug. On the table was an
open flask.

But now there came a fresh assault upon the
street door. Again I heard cries.

Chilenos? No, the rabble had gone their way.
Vigilantes? No, those mounted night patrolmen
were apparently quite indifferent to the fact of
my existence. The voices were familiar voices,
and the words were English.

"Hi there, boy! You in there, you rascal? Come, turn to! None o' your sogering! Do you hear the news? Tumble up, *lively!*" It was the old man!

I shouted back, "Spanish folks in here. Don't known English. Can't tell 'em to open the door!"

"Open it yourself, then, you leatherhead!" That was unmistakably the mate's voice.

Now my preservers, hearing English spoken and realizing that the men on the doorstep must be acquaintances of mine, or at all events no enemies, else I should have been afraid to answer, opened the door.

In strode the two burly men. The captain never looked so big, the mate was never so surly.

"Well," the old man observed in a tone of infinite disgust, "here you are with your head broke!"

My head was not exactly "broke," though it was by no means attractively embellished by my recent battle with the Personage. I had a gash about an inch long over my left eye, and that luckless optic was completely closed by the blackened swelling.

The old man roared at me with such thunderous ferocity that Inez was frightened. She seemed to think my destruction was now a matter of grim certainty. She threw herself upon her knees between the old man and his prey. Her mother at the same time seized the mate by the collar. It was like a scene in a melodrama!

I found the gust of cool night air from the open door very refreshing. There was a certain energizing property also in the old man's harsh voice. I rose from the couch. I felt so much better that I thought I could walk alone. I tried—yes, I could.

My first impulse was to kiss Inez (the dear girl!); but it occurred to me she would hardly like to be kissed by a chap with a broken head and a game eye. I found it somewhat easier to refrain from kissing her mother. I had not the slightest temptation to kiss the old man.

As it was, I bowed, and waved my hand in a futile sort of pantomime, and wished with all my heart I could put my farewell into words, for then I should have made Inez promise to write often. I was pitiably conscious of figuring in an awkward and inglorious attempt at sentiment. It was as absurd as that place in Fanny Burney's novel where it says, "They both wept, curtseyed and withdrew."

Very little was said about the affair, however, as we three Americanos returned to the *Swift*.

Of course I was wriggling with curiosity to know what in creation had become of Rudder Simpson and the Personage. I wanted to know, too, what had been the result of the fight and the subsequent riot. I suppose it was part of the old man's vengeful design to keep me in ignorance of the facts.

Next day, as I rose from my bunk, I was seized with a sudden fit of dizziness — from loss of blood, the old man said — and in consequence I was ordered to remain in bed all day.

I have always supposed that that was done in malice. The old man babied me there in port as you never saw him baby me at sea.

I spent that day imagining all possible and impossible outcomes of the affray. I sent Rudder to jail, had him tried for bloody murder and shot like a dog. I visited a similiar fate upon the Personage. I even congratulated myself that it had not been my own lot to leave my bones in the Potter's Field at Talcahuano. Over and over I turned the story till it became a sort of waking nightmare, growing constantly more and more hideous. I have heard of the fashionable woman who said she couldn't go to Europe because she was reading seventeen serial stories. My own interest in this Chileno romance was hardly less keen.

The day passed uneventfully, but late that
evening a shout went ringing through the ship,
calling all hands. All hands! And in port!
what possible emergency could occasion such an
appeal to force as that?

I leaped from my bunk, grabbed hastily for
boots and trousers, pulled them on in a jiffy, and
dashed up the cabin stairs. It was bright as day
only it was a horrible, yellow-red light. All was
confusion on deck. Orders were given in quick
succession. All hands were needed to save the
ship. I sprang up the ratlines with the rest. I
heard a voice say, " She's the *Ganges*, shipmates,
the *Ganges*, poor barky!" He was right. Off
to windward lay the handsome, well-found, full-
rigged ship *Ganges* of Fall River, swathed in a
shroud of flames.

In my excitement I obeyed orders automati-
cally, not stopping to consider the meaning of
the words I acted upon. Somehow I had got
the hollow of my feet set upon the foot-rope and
my arms flung over the particular yard assigned
me as my post of honor. I could see the *Ganges*
ablaze from stem to waist. A man at my right
was doing precisely what I was doing, waiting for
a bucket to be passed to him. The man had a
white nose. It was covered with sticking plaster.

"Why, Rudder," I exclaimed, "I didn't know you were alive!"

"Oh, yes," said the imperturbable Simpson. "Nose in a sling, but still seaworthy. Rigged up jury-nose — see?"

The fire burst through the *Ganges'* main-hatch, sending up a fountain of rushing, soaring, spreading, fluttering red sparks. They scattered out over the sky. They fell in hot showers upon a score of anchored ships. Every endangered vessel had men aloft.

Buckets were passed from tarry hand to tarry hand. We drenched the masts and yards and sails and rigging.

"Why in the name o' sea-sense, don't somebody scuttle the old hooker?"

"'Fraid to."

"Don't wonder; no fun to go below in a blazin' butter-box — resky, blamed resky. But why in blazes don't — — Oh, *look*, boy, *look!* clap yer for'ard lights on *that* — they done it a'ready!"

So they had. The old ballahoo settled away, like a spaded shark, and went hissing to the bottom, only her blazing masts still stuck out of the water.

"Good," said Rudder, "bully for every man Jack of 'em!"

Those various men Jacks were at that time
afloat in their whale-boats, and now they made for
a ship near by. The light had nearly faded away,
but we could still see them. In fact, we could
see the whole Bay of Conception, and the "long,
black land" six miles away across the harbor.

"Well," said Rudder, " s'pose the old man'll
keep us a-soakin' this here riggin' a good haour
more, blast 'im!"

"Then, Rudder," said I, "tell me how that
fight came out. I don't know a thing that happened after I was hit."

"Well," said Rudder, " 'tain't no great twister.
Chilenos an' mobs an' Dago police, an' the steward
o' that there *Ganges*, that's jest naow a-bunkin'
in Granny's wash-tub there, stuck in his blazin'
innards an' took to the haw-spittle, an' not a
blamed stitch o' liberty for them sweet, lob-lolly
boys sence! Them's the facts, boy."

"And what do you think now of that big
Chileno Personage — duke, baron, earl — some
such nabob?"

"Not by a jugfull! That there rainbow dandy,
so says Slush Dooley (an' he's knocked araoun'
Talky-wanno nigh onto a twelve-month), that
there rainbow dandy, says he, why, he's just a
darned old farmer. Them togs is what they wear

up-country. Blow all their cash on their jeans!
An' I tell you, boy, they ain't no true piosity in
splicin' elbows with Dago strangers — not of a
Sunday, no, sir — not if the court knows herself,
an' (feeling of his plastered nose, and glancing
mournfully at my bandaged head and blackened
eye) *she thinks she do!*"

We finally bade adieu to the beautiful islands
of the South Pacific ocean, and began our homeward voyage. We had a fair passage to the Cape,
but as we neared that point of storms and gales,
the days grew shorter and the weather more
boisterous. When we ran to the eastward, we
encountered heavy gales, with a tremendous sea
running. Although the gales were a fair wind
for us, the old man did not run nights, as the ship
was deeply laden with oil, and he was afraid of
losing our boats or having our decks swept by the
sea washing over us. We hove to several nights,
and on one of these nights we lost a man overboard. Thanks to the tireless exertions of the
crew, he was saved from a watery grave. He
had been sent aloft to loose the fore-top-sail
during the night and was stepping from the top-
sail yard to the rigging, when the ship fetched a
heavy roll to the windward. He missed his hold
and fell into the sea; but as he was to windward,

MAN OVERBOARD OFF CAPE HORN.

the sea washed him up to the side of the vessel, The night was very clear and the moon was full, so we could see the huge waves wash him up the ship's side and the receding wave, or undertow, take him away — sometimes fifty feet away. It would have been folly to attempt to lower a boat at that time. There was, however, only one other thing to do, and that we did. The men tied ropes around their bodies and hung over the side to grasp him if possible. After a while a sailor caught him by his foot, but his boot came off and we were almost ready to give him up as lost. Yet in a short time he was seen again, and was thrown to the side. Just at that moment one of our men seized him by the arm, and with help got him on board. The poor fellow was nearly done for, but by rubbing him, and wrapping him in warm blankets, and giving him hot drinks, we saved him. I have hinted at this story before. This was the man Townsend who tried to desert us at the Navigator Islands.

THE CAST-AWAY.

"Alone, alone ; all, all alone !
Alone on a wide, wide sea !"
— *Ancient Mariner.*

TRISTAN DE ACUNHA — ALMOST A WRECK.

"As beautiful Nancy was walkin' one dy,
  She met a young sylor, all hon the 'igh-wy,
'E stept up beside 'er, and to 'er did sy,
  O ware hare ye goin', tell me pretty myde ? "

" BULLY good ! " shouted a dozen gruff voices, " You sing like a gen'leman o' forshun ! Take 'nother turn around the capstan an' give us nex' versh ! "

" Close-reef, first," replied the Cockney singer. " Ware's the bloody bottle ? 'Ere, Weatherface, — the bottle, you lubber ! "

The British tar threw back his burly head and took an observation through his tumbler. He glanced round expectantly upon the crowd of whalemen, awaiting a more distinct *encore*.

" Nex' versh ! " roared Weatherface, making the low coral walls re-echo, " Nex' versh ! " Then they all shouted together, " Go on, Jack ! Go on ! "

So Jack Burkett took up his song again, sitting astride the canoe's bows in that abandoned boat-house, the light from a single lantern streaming warm and yellow in his hard face while he sang, —

> " As beautiful Nancy was walkin' one dy,
>   She met a young sylor, all hon the 'igh-wy,
> 'E stept up beside her," —

"Avast! Avast!" bawled Mattapoisett Joe, "Avast! you boozy lime-juicer, you 've sung that verse a 'ready. You 're half-seas over, lad. You 're drunk as old Weatherface."

" 'Old on, ye bloody Yank! Hif ye don't like me bloody chanty, then just ye sing us a bloody chanty as ye do like."

"The bottle," said Mattapoisett Joe, with a bland smile. "Will my brave friend Weatherface kindly pass me the bottle? First I'll splice the main-brace, and then I'll sing, as requested. Come, my bullies, we 'll all drink together! Fill up your glasses — how 's this for a toast? —

> ' Be cheery, my lads ! May your hearts never fail,
>   While the bold harpooneer is a-striking the whale !'

There, clink your glasses! — now shoot the sun!"

Up went twenty chins in air. Down went twenty scalding gulps of New England rum.

Mattapoisett set his empty tumbler on the coral window-sill, leaned heavily against the wall, folded his brawny arms, and began, — his round, mellow baritone filling the boat-house with a fine, vibrant melody. It was a voice that would have been worthy of applause in better company.

> "When sunk deep in sleep on the ocean,
> 'Neath southern skies' brilliant blue dome,
> In fancy I hear the trees rustle,
> That shaded my window at home.
> I hear the flocks bleat in the meadows,
> The cries of the men to their teams,
> But dearer to me are the many
> Loved faces I see in my dreams."

"Good, good, good!" they shouted, Britons and Yankees alike. Mattapoisett Joe had chosen the one song that would soften every heart, the "one touch of nature" that would make the whole sailor-world kin. He took up the second verse : —

> "First rises the old chimney corner,
> And then my dear father I see,
> Whose pride ties are over, are over,
> His children to have on his knee.
> And then by the bunk-board stands mother,
> With eyes full of sweet, loving joy,
> Who, ere going to rest, bends to offer
> A prayer for her poor sailor boy."

Had the light from the lantern been a very little brighter, all hands might have beheld real tears welling up in the eyes of Jack Weatherface, but whether his tender sentimentality was due to musical responsiveness, or to an affectionate disposition, or to a guilty conscience, or to the effects of New England rum, no fellow can say for certain. His feelings, however, were those of the whole company. The song had found their hearts.

Mattapoisett sang on, with a half perceptible quiver in his voice : —

> " All changeless beside me is standing,
>   A sweet girl I know, oh so well !
>   A voice murmurs, ' Break not your promise,
>   You made in the green, leafy dell ! '
>   Now she's gone ; and I start from my pillow,
>   Aroused by the sea-birds' wild screams,
>   And I'm far, far away from those loved ones,
>   Whose faces I see in my dreams ! "

There was a moment of silence.

Then " Bravo ! Bravo ! " burst from the throats of the whalemen.

The low rafters shook with their applause. Six tumblers were smashed in the uproar, and the sashing was knocked clean out of the window-frame.

" Come," said Mattapoisett, " Curse the doleful chanty ! Let's take a cruise around the old

French town! There's a bottle half-full. Put it under the canoe. When we come back we'll finish it off, and then *we'll* be half-full. eh. my hearties?"

With that the twenty ruffians burst through the door, — all but one, the English cooper. who, for half-inebriated reasons of his own. preferred to remain behind in the boat-house.

Now the palm wooded summit of "Mt. Blanc," looking down from the altitude of three thousand feet, has seen many a wild time in old Victoria. Often and often has the little island of Mahé, though biggest of all the Seychelles. been fairly made to shake under the riotous revelling of whaling crews ashore. But of all the fierce nights, this black and starless evening was among the fiercest; and of all the disorderly gangs ashore on Mahé. these Yankees of mine and these British tars from the "lime-juicer" were far to the fore.

"You know the old saw, ship-mates." sang out Mattapoisett Joe, "We must all hang together or we'll all hang separately!"

"Aye-aye," said Jack Burkett, "splice helbows heverybody. Hey, my lively 'earties. Splice helbows hall 'ands!"

And so they did; nineteen tipsy sailors all locking arms and careering wildly through the town.

7

They danced around a *gens d'armes*, they over-
turned a fruiterer's truck, they smashed a
dozen windows, and they kissed all the girls they
could find on the streets.   Then they locked arms
once more, and charged down the main avenue of
Victoria on their way back to the boat-house.

" Half bottle leff ! " gurgled poor, old Weatherface.   " Splice main brace, — brace main splice,—
close-reef ! "

As has already been intimated, the cooper of
the English whaleship, though absent, had not
been made conspicuous by his absence.   Now,
however, as the rollicking party tumbled into the
boat-house again, the cooper became shockingly
conspicuous by his presence.

He lay stretched out in the canoe, like the
Lady of Shalott, and he was quite as unconscious
as that unfortunate celebrity.   Beside him lay
the bottle (a " dead soldier ") entirely empty.

At first sight of so horrid a spectacle a howl of
dismay went up from the crowd.

" Blast   his   toppy   blood-lights ! "   r o a r e d
Weatherface.   " How'll we   main   splice-brace
now ? "

" Curse   the   cooper," said Burkett,   " *we'll*
cooper 'im; *we'll* put the 'oops on 'im; *we'll*
'ammer 'is styves ! "

But Mattapoisett was the recognized ring-leader. "Avast!" he cried, "See all clear! Shove them big doors open! We'll do for the son of a sea-cook! We'll do for him hand-some! Bear a hand there, my bully chummies, handsomely! Cheerily! Now, shipmates, all together!"

With that the ruffians seized hold of the cooper's canoe, rushed it swiftly down the beach, and launched it out into the darkness and the night.

Then they staggered back into their lair, shut the big doors, laid in a new bottle of "close-reef," drank the health of the cast-away cooper, and toasted his many virtues.

They topped off the barrel-smith's obsequies with that ghastly sailor-song since made famous by Stevenson:

"Fifteen men on the dead man's chest,
Yo-ho-ho, and a bottle of rum."

"Rum, rum, rum, an' bottle o' ho-ho!" mut-tered the hilarious Weatherface. "Let by-gones be 'gones! Somebody sing sholly janty!"

Burkett, so merry that he had quite forgotten his somewhat recent discomfiture, called lustily for a chanty from Mattapoisett Joe. The whole crowd took up the cry.

It was really wonderful what a cargo Matta-poisett could carry. He was a little uncertain in his steps, and he had an air of general inaccuracy that shook one's faith in his mental stability, yet his tongue had not forgotten its cunning.

The song as a song was a genuine triumph. Ah, yes; but the selection was most unfortunate. It was entitled "The Sailor's Grave," and ran like this : —

> "Our bark was far, far from the land,
>   When the fairest of our gallant band,
>   Grew deadly pale and weaned away,
>   Like the twilight hours of an autumn day.
>   We watched him through long hours of pain ;
>   Our cares were great, our hopes in vain.
>   At death's stroke he showed no coward alarms,
>   But smiled and died in his messmates' arms.
>
> "We had no costly winding-sheet,
>   We placed two-pound shot at his feet ;
>   He lay in his hammock as snug and proud
>   As a king in his long robe, marble bound.
>   We proudly decked his funeral vest,
>   With the stars and stripes across his breast —
>   We gave him these as a badge of the brave,
>   And then he was fit for a sailor's grave.
>
> "Our voices failed, our hearts grew weak,
>   Hot tears were seen on brownest cheek,
>   A quiver played on the lip of pride,
>   As we lowered him over the ship's dark side.
>   A plunge, and a splash, and it all was o'er,
>   The billows rolled as they rolled before ;
>   But many a wild prayer hallowed the wave,
>   As he sank to rest in a sailor's grave."

It may seem strange till you stop to think of it, but no applause rewarded the song. Each man had solemn and guilty thoughts in his heart, which were roused into terrible activity by Burkett's ill-chosen chanty. Yet no one spoke. The men were squatting on the boat-house floor, leaning lazily against the white walls. The yellow lantern was smoking dismally.

At this junction, so ominous of sullen resentment and its possible result in blows, if not bloodshed, a sudden interruption changed the scene abruptly.

There was a loud rapping on the door and cries of "*Ouvrez la porte, ouvrez aux gens d'armes, vous êtes nos prisonniers! Place aux officiers!*"

A dozen uniformed Frenchmen, armed to the teeth, dashed into the boat-house; great confusion ensued; several pistol-shots were fired into the air; there were grapplings and blows here and there; and then the biggest of the *gens d'armes*, no doubt a sort of prefect of police, screamed out in broken English, "Silence! *Je* command silence; you think you *pouvez* raise *le diable* in zis place! You think you *pouvez* embrace *tous les dames!* I tell you non, *non,* NON, *messieurs!*"

Amazed at the brilliant behavior of the prefect, the whalemen " came to order." In an instant the boathouse seemed transformed from a field of battle to a court of justice.

Mattapoisett pleaded for the whole crowd, urging that his followers were a well-meaning lot of lads; gentle little things, you know, and very young; and that they were not altogether familiar with the customs of Mahé, and had offended unwittingly. How were an innocent crew of foreigners to know that the ladies of Victoria objected to being promiscuously kissed? In New Bedford, he insisted, it was so different. They were very, very sorry, and would never, never, never disturb the island again.

The upshot of the matter was that the drunken sailors were all shipped off to the whalers in the harbor; and, thanks to Mattapoisett's logic and rhetoric, no arrests were made. However a *gens d'armes* came aboard the *Hope* to notify me that my crew had received an official reprimand, and from the *Hope* he went directly to the captain of the lime juicer.

" *Ciel!* " he said, " *Vos hommes, ne sont-ils pas méchants ?* "

Now, when the English officers counted noses next morning, they found many a grog-blossomed bill, but there were not quite bills enough to suit them. Some one was missing.

There was no cooper to be found amongst the crew !

Apparently the cooper had deserted; or was it not possible that he had been arrested and jailed for participation in the night's disturbances? In either case there was but one thing to do — appeal to the authorities on shore.

This the bold Briton reluctantly did, hating above all things to ask a favor of a Frenchman. At the same time he sent off a boat to call at every ship in the harbor and request that diligent search for the missing cooper be made on board. The day went by; the whole island and the whole harbor were searched with the utmost care; but the lost sheep could nowise be brought back into the fold.

A council extraordinary met in the forecastle of of the lime juicer that afternoon and chose Jack Burkett as their unwilling spokesman, deputing him to proceed to the quarter-deck and to render to the captain a full and complete confession of their manifold sins and wickednesses, neither dissembling nor cloaking them, but acknowledging them all "with an humble, lowly, penitent and obedient heart."

So Burkett went aft upon the hateful errand. He told the whole disgraceful story — nineteen sailors crazy with rum, the English cooper set adrift in an oarless and paddleless canoe, and a strong tide running out to the ocean.

Rage like that of a frenzied demon blazed from the old man's tough countenance. He swore a volley of terrible curses.

But as soon as he came to himself he realized that not a moment was to be lost in the mere indulgence of righteous wrath; so, calling "'Hall 'ands" aft, he detailed the men to various duties in rescue service.

The mast-heads were to be manned directly. Two boats were to spread the news through the harbor and ask assistance in the name of humanity. The other boats were to sail and row out to sea as far as they dared and with all speed, keeping wide apart, to cover as large an area as possible, and search for the cooper's canoe.

I gladly lent my services in so imperative an enterprise. I was the more eager to help find the cooper because, years and years before, I had seen a cooper buried at sea, and my sympathies were touched and my fears aroused by the recollection of that pitiful scene. Was the poor English barrel-smith to be lost in the deep, buried in its restless waters, and not to be honored with even the formal reading of a written service?

It is strange with what vividness such impressions live in one's memory, and upon what slender grounds of suggestion they rise anew into activity.

It seemed but as yesterday that we had left Talcu-
huano for a cruise on the coast of Chili, and we
were only a few days from port when our cooper
fell violently ill. We were within a day's sail of
Valparaiso, so the old man steered for that port
and went on shore for medical advice. He
returned with some medicine, but it proved of
no avail. Next day the cooper died. We kept
him till the following afternoon, and then we
buried him.

At four o'clock the ship's headway was stopped.
the stars and stripes flung out at half-mast, and all
hands called to bury the dead. Wrapped in his
blanket and sewed in strong canvas. with a bag of
sand ballast at his feet, the dead man's body was
brought to the waist and laid gently on the gang-
way board. As the captain read the solemn
service, the men uncovered and bowed their heads.
At the words "We commit his body to the deep,"
the pall-bearers lifted the body slowly at the head;
and then — all that remained to us of our shipmate was the pleasant memory he left behind him,
for he had always been a favorite among our crew.
So we left him to his peaceful, dreamless sleep,
"there to await the general resurrection in the
last day." That night I read with a better
understanding the cheering words of the Apostle,

A BURIAL AT SEA.

"This mortal shall put on immortality." (You didn't know they had Bibles on whale-ships? Yes, they do; and what's more, they read them.) I had witnessed many burials on shore, but none had ever impressed itself so indelibly upon my mind as this solemn burial at sea.

Nor was this the only tragical recollection that haunted my mind as we joined in that heart-breaking search for the castaway.

For my thoughts went out to a certain place upon the northern end of Bird Island, one of this same Seychelles Group — a spot I have ever since called the mournfullest as well as the most desolate place in the whole world. There, grouped together upon a lonely, sun-beaten flat, whose stillness is broken only by the heavy, rolling surf that dashes on the shore, are the graves of a dozen sailors who have been buried from whale-ships cruising around those banks for whales.

Once more I seemed to be standing alone among those uncared-for graves, and looking out across the waste of waters toward the distant home, thinking I could see some poor mother waiting and longing and watching, and at last so grievously disappointed; or perhaps a wife and her little children, enduring prolonged separation from the one best loved of all, because they are saying, "It can't be much longer, dearie, — it *can't* be *much* longer!"

Then was this poor English cooper to be denied even so desolate a resting-place as the sailor's cemetery on Bird Island?

And who — I could not help asking — who would be the broken-hearted ones at home? Who would listen with grief and with tears to the shameful story of the drunken castaway and his tragical end? Oh, there would be sorrow and mourning in that little English hamlet on the Devonshire coast! Not tonight, nor tomorrow night; but a whole year hence, it might be, or even longer, when the tale would be told at home by the very men who had sent the cooper to his doom.

Darkness settled like a pall upon our disheartening enterprise. The stars, blazing down from that southern sky, glared pitiless and cruel. The moon — red, sullen, mockingly splendid — rose out of the ocean and made a broad, straight path to the horizon. (Out upon that path, the men said, the cooper's canoe had gone.) "Mt. Blanc" loomed black in the far distance. We could still see the lights on the ships in the harbor, though the lights of the town had already sunk into the sea.

At last we turned back and went aboard the whalers. We had satisfied ourselves that the cooper had ere this met his death.

There was grief and remorse aboard the *Hope*. Half our men had *murder* written red across their souls.

All the next day the crew brooded and repented and growled. There were no songs in the forecastle. There was no mention of " The Sailor's Grave." There was no allusion to faces seen in dreams. They had all seen the same face. Nor was there any inclination to go ashore. The town was a haunted town, the boat-house a haunted house. The men longed to leave port. In the changeless routine of sailing or the adventurous vicissitudes of whale-hunting, they could forget their crime.

And so even the third day went by much as had the others before it, though there was a lively scuffle in the forecastle late that afternoon. Mattapoisett Joe was knocked down and jumped upon by three of his shipmates.

When I looked into the matter I found that Mattapoisett had been assaulted as a punishment for — what do you think? — whistling! A trivial offense, you say. Yes, but listen.

" You can't blame us, sir," said Weatherface, when all hands had been called aft for the investigation. "He was whistling the tune of that devilish song, —

> "'Fifteen men on the dead man's chest,
>   Yo‑ho‑ho, and a bottle of rum.'

If you was us, you'd jumped on him, too, sir!"

I turned to the bruised whistler, and I said, "Joe, my man, what shall I do to these lads?"

"Let 'em all go, sir," said Mattapoisett, "I got no more 'n I deserved."

"Now go forward, every man of you," said I, "and let me hear no more of your troubles."

I say the third day went by. Perhaps that is an over-statement. As my men started forward, the sun was already setting. The whole harbor was red in its glare.

No sooner had the crew left the quarter-deck than loud cheers were heard off to starboard. The men on the British whaler were dancing about like lunatics, pitching their caps into the air, and shouting themselves hoarse.

"'Urrigh! 'Urrigh!! 'Urrigh!!!" they yelled. "'Ere's for the cooper, once more, boys, — 'Urri-i-i-igh!"

A tiny fishing smack had been beating up the harbor for the last hour, and now she was coming alongside the lime-juicer. Once within hailing distance, her skipper had cried out to the British captain, " Ahoy, *monsieur!* Ahoy! *J'ai votre coopier!* "

No cooper was seen, but the cooper's canoe followed close in the wake of the sloop.

Just then two heads appeared above the fisherman's hatch-way. A moment more, and a third head came in view.

It was the cooper — pale and sick and haggard. but still alive — carried in the arms of his preservers.

" Hurray! Hurray! " our sailors answered when they fully took in the situation. Then they danced as wildly as the Englishmen, hugged each other like school-girls, and all but wept for joy.

" Hip, hip! " shouted Mattapoisett Joe, forgeting his bruises.

" Hurr-a-a-a-a-a-a-y! ! ! ! " yelled the whole crew, and I yelled with them.

That night after supper I gave orders to my men to put on their Sunday clothes, and to dress our boats with all the bunting they could carry.

Weatherface was to bring his fiddle or be put in irons. Little Tom Bunker was to bring his accordion or suffer a similar penalty. The cabin-boy, a mere creeper on the face of the earth, was to remain behind as ship-keeper.

Then we manned the boats, lowered away, and pulled to the merry lime-juicer.

We found ourselves no unexpected guests. Elaborate preparations had been made for our entertainment. The "doctor" had filled his "coppers" with the most toothsome of land fare. The crew had dressed up to receive us. The ship had been loaded with bright-colored bunting. The decks had been cleared for dancing. There was an all-round, rollicking, sailorly good time that lasted till midnight.

The poor cooper, though fully conscious of the honors being paid him, was too weak and wretched to join in the festivities. A doctor from on shore came off to look at him, and recommended hot milk as a harmless restorative. When I looked in upon the cooper the poor fellow turned his head mournfully on his pillow and said, "Shiver my soul, but I feel like a 'ard-boiled owl!"

Next morning we hoisted our Blue Peter, a homeward bounder. It was worth a cask of sperm oil to hear our crew sing at the windlass as they hove up anchor. I was an old sea-dog even in those days; I didn't come through the cabin windows; I was put through the mill, ground and bolted; but never in all my long and varied salt-water experience had I heard a crew sing better.

Mattapoisett's resonant baritone carried the solo lines superbly. The crew shouted the refrain with spirit — or, as little Tom Bunker said, " with great venom."

"My boy he was a sailor, he sailed away to sea,
   Heave away, my hearties; heave away, my boys!
" But when he went to sea he vow,d he'd soon come back to me!
   Heave away, my hearties; heave away, my boys!
" He sailed upon a vessel, a-whaling for to go,
   Heave away, my hearties; heave away, my boys!
" It was a tedious journey, but he was bound to go,
   Heave away, my hearties; heave away, my boys!
" The captain was a good man, a sailor to the core,
   Heave away, my hearties; heave away, my boys!
" T'was early in the morning, the watch was down below,
   Heave away, my hearties; heave away, my boys!
" A sailor in the mainmast crow's-nest sang out 'There she blows!'
   Heave away, my hearties, heave away, my boys!
" They lowered the boats and struck the whale, and soon the
      monster died,
   Heave away, my hearties; heave away, my boys!
" They tied a rope upon him tight, and towed him alongside,
   Heave away, my hearties; heave away, my boys!
" We cut him in and tried him out, and stowed him down below,
   Heave away, my hearties; heave away, my boys!
" We'll set all sail, and head her straight, and homeward we will go,
   Heave away, my hearties; heave away, my boys!
" And soon we shall be home again; our friends we soon shall see,
   Heave away, my hearties; heave away, my boys!
" And when we see New Bedford, we will no more go to sea,
   Heave away, my hearties; heave away, my boys!
" And when we go 'longside the wharf, and put our feet on shore,
   Heave away, my hearties; heave away, my boys!
" You can gamble that we'll never go a-whaling any more,
   Heave away, my hearties; heave away, my boys!"

It was just about Christmas time, fine hot weather, that we came within sight of Tristan de Acunha, Lat. 37° S., and Long. 12° 16' W. The

8

THE BARK "HOPE" TOWING OFF TRISTAN DE ACUNHA ISLAND.

Portuguese discoverer, whose name the island bears, put in his first appearance, so I have read, in 1506. He certainly deserves to have his name thus immortalized for he gave the world a new treasure, indeed — a very pearl of an island, seven miles across, as round as a dollar, and enclosing a fresh-water lake which never freezes. That, no doubt, is explained by the volcanic nature of the whole formation. Cliffs, straight as a castle wall, tower up from the water's edge to a height of two thousand feet. Harbor there is none, and but for a narrow inlet on the north side, no adequate landing place. A group of white-washed stone houses on the north-west shore is the nearest approach to a town anywhere on the island.

Now the reason all these details have fastened themselves so tenaciously upon my memory is that right here I came near losing my ship. It was late in the afternoon, and we were taking off supplies from the shore. The wind — our only stay since it was too deep water for our best bower to touch bottom — had died out to a calm. It was an Irishman's hurricane, straight up and down; and yet the strong ground-swell of the ocean kept carrying us further and further in shore. We cracked on every stitch of canvas we

could spread, and with half a hand at the billows
we should have forged ahead all fluking ; but as it
was, our sails hung as limp as the dangling damp
sheets on an indoor clothes-horse.   There was not
a bubble of white water at our prow.   There was
not a streak or ripple in our wake.   And yet
moment by moment those awful cliffs grew taller.
We sent out a boat with a line — then two boats
— then three ! — trying our sturdiest to ratch the
precious barky out of imminent danger.   At last
the cliff-crests seemed to rise no higher, though
we dared not trust our eyes, we so longed to see
them stop rising.   Already the breakers pounded
ominously at their feet.   Already the sea-birds,
nesting amongst their crags, called hideously near.

By chance — or rather, as I have always said,
by the providence of God — another ship — and
she a whaler, lay not far from us.   I set my colors
for assistance, and down into the water came her
boats, the davit-blocks creaking and the whalemen shouting encouragement to our three boats'
crews.   Swift as so many racers in a regatta, the
stranger's cedar craft came ripping through the
smooth water, every dip and plash of their oars
seeming measurably to lift and lighten the burden
of our suspense.   Six boats and thirty-six men
saved the *Hope* from being sent on that iron-

bound shore. We towed her well off shore, and a tardy flaw of wind at last bellied out her canvas. Then is it any wonder that I have never forgotten Tristan de Acunha?

THE WHALEMAN WHO WENT ON THE STAGE.

" Being in a ship is being in jail, with a chance of being drowned."
— Dr. Samuel Johnson.

JOHN PIERCE certainly came down from aloft. There could be no possible doubt about that. I certainly spoke with him as he passed me on his way to the forecastle. This much, I am sure, will never be called in question.

But what followed — even to this hour it makes me shudder, sickened with dread, to recall what followed — the days of anxiety, the grim mystery, the final despair, and the haunting, harrowing problem of that tragical disappearance!

We had put in at Fayal to ship home some hundred barrels and more of sperm oil, and then cleared away and steered to the south, carrying all sail to get away from the island. We left at five in the afternoon, and by eleven o'clock that night, when we had made about fifteen miles offing, I gave orders to take in our top-gallant sails, and poor Pierce went aloft with the others. As he slid down the backstay and passed me on deck, I had a pleasant word with him, and then he went forward and was lost to view in the darkness. Many a time since then have I had reason to be glad that my last words to the man were kind.

At four next morning, when the watch was called, no John Pierce could be found.

Every nook and every smallest cranny in the whole ship was looked into, but all to no purpose. Not a trace of the fellow could we discover. Reluctantly at last we gave him up as lost, convinced against our wills that he had tumbled overboard during the night.

A solemn hush fell upon us. Hardened, though most of us were, and accustomed to the constant dangers of a seaman's calling — used though we were to these sudden disappearances from life and duty — we could never be reconciled to them. Indeed, it seemed as if each new death of this sort were more dreadful than the one before it.

But, as usual, the sense of shock and of wrong went by. The man's absence ceased to impress us. At last we had almost forgotten the circumstance of his taking off.

About one year from the night of Pierce's disappearance, we were cruising off Madagascar.

I happened that day to be running over my log-book and chanced upon the entry of the facts noted above. There was the record in my own hand, a deep border of black drawn around it. I found that I had departed from the usual dry and formal log-book style. Indeed, I had sentimental-ized not a little. Viewing, in calmer mood, this eulogy of John Pierce, I could not help feeling a little amused. I had always made fun of funeral sermons, and here I had been preaching one myself in black and white.

As I was in the midst of this reverie, the cabin-boy dropped down the stairway to bring word that a whale-ship had just been sighted. It was not long after that, with customary ceremonies, we spoke her. She proved to be an old friend from Sag Harbor.

We kept fairly close together until sundown, and then the Sag Harbor captain and boat's crew came on board to spend the evening.

There in the boat, to our utter amazement, was JOHN PIERCE! He had grown a stubby beard since last we had seen him, but that was no dis-guise. There he was (to my infinite relief) alive and well — the same unmistakable, happy - go - lucky, jolly Jack Tar as before he had gone to his watery grave. It was enough to make a man believe in the transmigration of souls! I was mightily glad to see him alive, though, to tell the truth, I had not greatly missed his services.

We got a part of the story from the Sag Harbor captain. It seems they had sailed out of port about ten in the morning, the next day after Pierce's strange disappearance. At four that afternoon, when they were about fifteen miles from the land, the man at the lookout on the mainmast head reported something in sight, floating on the water about two miles from the ship. The captain went aloft with the glass to have a look at it, but could not make out what it was, only he was certain it was something alive, for it kept moving and wriggling all the while, as if to attract attention from the ship. The old man's curiosity was so thoroughly aroused by this time that he veered off his course and steered straight for the strange object.

"When I came near enough," said the captain, "What should I see through my glass but a little live man, squatting on the surface of the water and waving his arms! Yes, that's the real truth, and I give an honest seaman's word for it."

My eyes were well open by this time, and I was beginning to believe the story.

Talk about mermaids and sea-serpents and the Flying Dutchman and the rest of the fo'cas'le nonsense! Here was a real, genuine thing to beat 'em all!

"But the lad's aboard now. Here, John Pierce, come into the cabin, my man, and tell Captain Robbins the stiffest twister he ever listened to! Come, make a clean breast of it. Tell us how you proved yourself the fool-hardiest, daredevilest galley-growler that ever earned a sailor's blessing!"

Pierce had already come, unwilling and with much hesitation, through the cabin door. Apparently he was gladder to see me than he was to have to talk with me.

"Give us your flipper, boy; how are you?" said I.

Pierce grinned sheepishly. "Oh, I'm all right," he answered, "right enough anyhow for a fellow that's been a whole good year in the bottom of the sea."

"Come, come," said the captain, "out with it! Tell the whole outrageous yarn from beginning to end or I'll log you, haze you, clap the darbies on your wrists, make a spread eagle of you, and invite you to walk the plank; and then if that won't do, I'll shut you up in the run and feed you on bread and water!"

We laughed, all three, and the bashful Pierce sat down between the two "old men" and took up his parable.

"Fact is," he began reluctantly, "Stormy Jones and I got sick 'o the voyage. Nothin' personal, Cap'n, only we just thought we'd got to have a change.

"So I says to Jones, 'shipmate,' says I, 'let's move!'

"'Avast,' says he, 'where the deuce'll we move to?'

"Then says I to Jones, 'Stormy,' says I, 'you know them stages?'

"'What o' them stages?' Jones asks, never taking my meaning.

"Then I says to Jones, 'Bear a bob, messmate, till I tell you the news. This is what we'll up and do. We'll lower one of them stages over the ship's bows in the middle o' some dark night and we'll float away on it, us two, and before we're old and gray and toothless some ship or other'll come along and' pick us up.'

"'Risky,' says Jones.

"'Aye, aye, sir,' says I, 'Its risky, maybe, and risky maybe not. Ships go in schools like cow whales on these here grounds. Say we try it, my man!'

"Then Stormy agrees, old hypocrit as he is, and next thing you know he goes and backs out of it, and I finds myself turned captain and mate

and crew and cabin-boy of a craft eight feet long
and just fifteen inches wide.   But I says to myself,
' Pierce, you fool, you're in for it now, so trust
to luck for your miserable life.   If you don't
do the act that Jones will tell the crew, and then
you'll have hell afloat the rest of the voyage.

" Well, Cap'n Robbins, you remember that
night I took my leave.   You thought I'd gone
overboard, didn't you ?   You was dead right, cap'n,
dead right, right as a right whale.   That's just
where I *had* gone.   But you thought I'd lost the
number of my mess, and in that you were all
wrong ! "

I stared at Pierce, my eyes big with wonder.
The Sag Harbor captain stared at me, a broad
grin covering his hard red face as he watched me
take in this ridiculous confirmation of his story.

I said nothing.

" Go on, Pierce," said Pierce's captain.

" Well," said the sailor, " you've got most of the
yarn a'ready, sir.   But, O Lord ! how my heart
sickened when I heard that stage go plunk into
the water on the *Pope's* bow.   Then I slipped
down onto it and let go.   It was all I could do
not to holler for help as the stage slipped aft in
the swash.   Oh, but I was sick o' the job !   After
awhile I *did* holler, but it was too late.   Nobody

could hear me. Then I says, 'Pierce, my hearty, you'll never'll see your Nancy!'

"You know the rest. The cap'n here picked me up when I was as hungry as a polar bear, and deathly faint and scared and discouraged.

"But what beats me, Cap'n Robbins, is that Jones held his tongue all that while and never told you the news; for if ever a seaman was rigged with self-acting jawing tackle, it's that same lubberly coward of a stormy Jones!"

This ended the mighty yarn. The Sag Harbor man beamed red as a sunset.

"Aha, sir," said he, "you thought I could swear through a nine-inch plank, didn't you? But it's true, every word, just as I tell you and just as my man Pierce has said. And, Pierce, if the Cap'n has no objections, you may go for'ard and see if you can't find some of your old shipmates in the fo'cas'le."

"Pierce," I added, "when you feel like it, you may come back here and read your epitaph in the log-book. You'll never recognize it as your own, I'll warrant."

Then the Sag Harbor man lit his pipe, leaned back in his chair, crossed his stout legs, and changed the subject. "By the way, Cap'n," said he, " what do you hear from New Bedford ? They tell me its the busiest station on the Underground Railroad."

"WHALES HAS FEELIN'S."

" Whales has feelin's as well as anybody. They don't like to be stuck in the gizzards, an' hauled alongside, an' cut in, an' tried out in these here boilers no more'n I do!" — *Barzy Mack's Biology.*

THE whale having gone down, we waited for him to come up again. Three boats danced idly upon the warm Madagascan water — the mate's, the second mate's and my own. The sun blazed viciously down from a cloudless sky.

We lay well apart, covering a large area of swelling, billowy sea. When the whale came up again, the real battle would begin.

A whole hour we waited in anxious expectance. As is natural at such times, my thoughts, meanwhile, ran back years and years to other whales and other fights. Once when I was a cabin boy I had stood three hours in the stern of a stoven boat, sunk just to the gunwale, while two wounded whales were cutting about and making the water white with their huge flukes, so near that it seemed they must kill me. Was the monster, down below in those vague amethystine depths, preparing some such terrors for the present occasion? I recalled, too, how once a dying whale had brought his spout-hole up against our boat

and belched barrelsfull of gore all over us, so that
when I opened my eyes every man was painted
red — completely covered with fresh, hot blood,
so that we all jumped into the water for a hasty
bath.   Was this sunken leviathan making ready
to serve us thus today ?   I also remembered how
a gigantic spouter had tossed me on his flukes
— boat, boat's crew, craft and all — *whist !* —
twenty feet into the air, till it seemed that we'd
never come down ; and how I found myself at
last launched adrift, clinging to a piece of the
steering-oar, which had snapped off at the stern-
post of the shattered boat.   Had not *this* whale
flukes also ?   How would he use them ?   Should
I be his victim ? or the mate ? or the third mate ?

There is something delicious in this exciting
uncertainty.   It makes your blood tingle.   It
makes your nerves thrill.   It makes you feel
yourself ready to face the whole world of perils
and proudly conquer them all.   You stand in the
stern-sheets, leaning on the steering-oar, and as
you look into the faces of those five stalwart men
on the thwarts before you, you tell yourself they
are fine heroes, every man Jack of them.   Yes,
heroes !   Soldiers face no greater perils.   Soldiers
win no worthier laurels.   Back of every trophy of
military valor, you must needs see human blood-

shed, human bereavement, human cruelty, and, far too often, the human lust for name and place. But the whaleman's glories are sullied by no such shameful pollution. Is he rich when his sea-toiling days are done? He has impoverished no one. Instead, he has added to the world's wealth. Is he successful in the pursuit of his calling? No widow and no tearful orphans mourn over his triumphs. Is he proud of his profession? He can claim for it the good name of an honest livelihood, a lawful and law-abiding business, a field for soldierly courage purged of soldierly brutality. Nor do tyrany and oppression follow in his paths. Instead, come only the blessings of a peaceful prosperity.

So, as I was saying, you stand and wait, a-tingle with enthusiasm. You are in your glory now. You would not for the whole world be any other thing but a whaleman. You are glad that your boyhood anticipated this splendid life of adventure, and aspired after its high responsibilities. To its toils and its perils you willingly devote your youth and best manhood. You will be proud, in long years to come, to recount the history of your daring sea-battles.

Few landsmen can understand these things. You must go a-blubber-hunting on your own account, fully to grasp their meaning. In fact I know of only one land-lubber who ever really caught the spirit of the whale-hunt, and that is old Walt Whitman, who wrote those splendid, pictorial lines (albeit they go devoid of rhyme, and, in place of precise metre, have only a feeble and slovenly wobble):

" O the whaleman's joys! O I cruise my old cruise again!
I feel the ship's motion under me, I feel the Atlantic breezes
    fanning me.
I hear the cry again sent down from the mast-head, *There she
    blows !*
Again I spring up the rigging to look with the rest — we descend,
    wild wi'h excitement,
I leap in the lowered boat, we row toward our prey where he lies,
We approach stealthy and silent, I see the mountainous mass,
    lethargic, basking, .
I see the harpooner standing up, I see the weapon dart from his
    vigorous arm ;
O swift again far out in the ocean the wounded whale, settling,
    running to windward, tows me.
Again I see him rise to breathe, we row close again,
I see a lance driven through his side, pressed deep, turned in the
    wound,
Again we back off, I see him settle again, the life is leaving him
    fast.
As he rises he spouts blood, I see him swim in circles narrower and
    narrower, swiftly cutting the water —
I see him die.
He gives one convulsive leap in the centre of the circle, and then
    falls flat and still in the bloody foam."

Barring the single sentence " I see the mountainous mass," (apparently Whitman thought a whale cruised around two-thirds out of water, like

a steam-boat) that is a perfect description of the
taking of the whale. It is more than that. It is
the picture of the inner experience of the chase
and the fight — the joy of it, the glow of it, the
wild, fierce thrill of it!

I was wishing with all my heart, as we waited
for that submarine lounger to return to the surface, that I could somehow tell which boat would
get a chance to fasten to him.

But a sudden end to reminiscence and philoso-
phizing. Look! There is frantic excitement in
the mate's boat off to leeward — " Stand up and
give it to him! Quick, quick, *quick*!" See! — a
figure erect in the boat's bow — a long shaft
wielded in both hands high over the man's head —
a momentary poise — a swift, springing motion —
a sudden recoil — the harpoon hurtling through the
air—the slender line singing after it—the weapon
sunk fast in something, and that something
sinking rapidly into the depths, dragging the line
through the chocks so fast the druggs could do
nothing to steady it — fifty fathoms — a hundred — two hundred! The mate and the harpooner have changed places. The men dodged
the flying line.

Now followed a fresh period of suspense —
anxious, but brief.

After a few minutes, there was a sudden uproar in the second mate's boat. Again the excited cry, "Stand up *quick — give* it to him! ! Again a heavy harpoon was sent a-whizzing through the air, and plunging deep into that awful, water-hidden something. Again the confusion in the boat and the preparation for lancing.

Responsive to the stab of this second harpoon, the monster sullenly settled under water. The battle was now well joined. What next?

'Suddenly and all unexpected, the whale came up again like a submarine boat. He bumped his back against the blades of the first mate's oars. His shiny black hump stood fully a foot out of water. The men could feel the damp heat of his spout. We could hear the sound of it.

This time old Blubber had gore in his eye. He was in for carnage and calamity and consternation. He lifted his huge square nose ten feet into the air, and dropping his long under-jaw, deliberately calculated his distance. Then with a hideous swing of his whole appalling mass, he veered round and took that whale-boat into his mouth. His ivory teeth smashed through the cedar clinker-work. The boat went to pieces like an egg-shell.

The mate's crew flung themselves headlong into the water, and escaped by the skin of their teeth.

THE FIGHTING WHALE.

Now the whale turned suddenly about. His rage redoubled. He would have blood or die for it. Making for the third officer's boat, he threw his cruel jaw across it, turning it bottom-up and staving it in. Again, as by a miracle, every man escaped unhurt.

A pretty situation! There were now two boats' crews floundering and sputtering in the water, while the whale was lashing the waves into froth with his flukes and sending the suds flying in every direction.

With the one remaining boat, I succeeded in picking up the swimmers, and in ferrying them away to the ship. Fortunately we had not far to travel.

How beautiful the *Clara Bell* looked as the boat came round so that I faced her again! Never had I thought her graceful, half-clipper lines such an exquisitely perfect model. Never had winged-dragon figure-head impressed me as such a consummate triumph of the wood-carver's art. Never had the two white streaks along her side from stem to stern seemed such a splendid decoration. Never, in all the days I had sailed in her, had she looked the white-robed angel-guardian she did now. She stood with her main-yard hauled aback. She nodded and dipped, and rose jauntily on the ocean swell. She was the joyfullest ship on all the seas. We were going back to her

"Oh, ain't I all-fired glad we got done with that wild-eyed monster?" The speaker was dripping with brine. "I calc'lated I was clean daown-swallered like old Jonah — all-fired sure I were!"

"Maybe I ain't glad, too! oh, maybe not! I could look way down in the dratted brute's dratted big gizzards. Deep? Maybe not. Oh, no. Felt like I was dangled over the drattedest deep pit in the whole dratted world."

"*I* wouldn't touch that there man-eater with the far-end of a spare yard — not for *money*;" said a third, squeezing the salt-water out of his beard, "no, not for money. I tell you, mess-mates, it's homicide an' man-slaughter, an' bloody murder with malice aforethought to take an' dump two boats' crews down the gullet o' that pesky man-eater, *I* tell you!"

But think not, gentle reader, that these words were spoken in anything graver than jest.

That this whale was a tough one, I have no inclination to deny — not the slightest. I followed the sea forty-one years, I was captain of a ship twenty-eight years, I have sailed more than a million miles, and I have had a hand in the taking of about twelve thousand barrels of oil; but this fighting leviathan off Fort Dauphin was one of the fiercest bits of blubber I ever raised out of the ocean. Yet neither I nor my men had any thought of surrender. We had already wasted two boats on him and we meant to be paid for the outlay. We insisted upon exacting a war indemity, payable in sperm oil — a hundred or a hundred and twenty barrels — the more the merrier!

We clambered up the ship's side and over the rail. From the deck we could get a startling view of the enemy. The infuriated beast lay wounded, only a short distance from the ship, thrashing around amongst the floating *debris* — oars, paddles, lanterns, and water-kegs — to say nothing of what remained of our two boats, the one a stoven wreck, the other smashed to splinters. It would have turned a landsman cold and stiff with horror. Nor am I certain that all our crew were anxious to renew the battle.

Be that as it may, we immediately got down two new spare boats from the skids overhead. We made them ready for a desperate encounter as we were going into the face of death. We meant to have the chances in our favor. The boats must be made as light as possible, so as to be able to dart away in an instant, if necessary, when the whale showed fight again. To this end,

we hastily prepared the most severely abridged
outfit — not an inch of line, and not a single piece
of craft beyond a gun and a bomb-lance in the
mate's boat and two hand-lances in mine. We
manned the boats with strong crews. The mate
took the second mate along with him, and I took
the third mate. We lowered the boats and sped
away toward our prey.

How bright, how amber-hued, the southern
sunlight, as it fell languorous and beautiful upon
the ocean billows! How buoyant the dance of our
hurrying boats! How impressive the swoop and
the soaring of the white gulls and albatrosses!
And yet, I dare say, not one of us responded to
the fine romanticism of nature — we were bent
upon too desperate an errand. There may be a
perennially fascinating charm in whaling life when
viewed from afar, but there are times when the
business assumes a grim ugliness at close range.
The poetry of the sea has always been written by
landsmen. It always will be.

Charm assuredly there had been in the suspense
and expectant anxiety preceeding this desperate
fight — charm enough, when its horrors were only
a possibility; but *now*, when the mystery was
pierced, the terrors become hideous facts, and the
nature of the foe fully known, the fun was gone

altogether.　When a fighting whale has chewed up two of your boats and beaten you roundly in his first pitched battle, it is a little unpleasant to go at him again.

Our blood ran high, as we approached the infuriated monster.　His spout stood up as tall as ever.　He had been no whit enfeebled by his tremendous exertions.　Two harpoons stuck out of his back.　His flukes swung in air with deadly force and rapidity.

The mate went to leeward of him and fired a bomb-lance into him, but missed his vitals.

Instantly the wounded creature turned about, heaved his head way out of water, opened his cavernous mouth, and made a frightful lunge for the mate's boat.　I was just in time.　I stood in the bow of my boat, hardly able to wait long enough to choose the right spot for the stab.　I was mad with excitement.　I plunged the long lance deep into the whale's vitals, and the blood came belching out of his spout-hole rich and red and warm, and after a few moments our victim turned up dead and in a few moments more we had him in the fluke chains along side the *Clara Bell*.

Deafening indeed were the cheers from the ship's deck when we had won that desperate

fight; warm was the hand-grip of mess-mates as
we climbed aboard; broad and bland the smile on
every sun-browned face! We were all alive. We
were all unhurt. We had killed the whale.

The inevitable well-worn joke now went the
rounds. "Better have paid your wash-woman!"

"*You* needn't talk, Jack; you're as wet as a
draownded shark."

"Don't care if I be. Ain't no gearin' 'tween
wash-tubs an' whale-boats. Who said there was?"

"*You* did, you slushy hypocritter, you. Ef
'taint so, then what'd you say I cheated my
wash-woman for, jest on accaount o' me bein' in a
stoven boat, you loony beach-comber?"

"Clew down your jawin'-tackle, sonnywax!
Cheerily, oh!"

This sort of mock-malice stood for the best of
good-will. The more those men berated each
other the better they felt all around.

When they took the falls to the windlass and
manned the bars it was a joy to hear them sing.
Sailor-songs are not metrically faultless, any more
than Whitman's poems; but they have the Jack
Tar spirit of the forecastle breathing all through
them, and hear and there a touch of easy humor.
This particular song ran, as I remember it, something after this fashion : —

" O, Johnny was no sailor,
 (Renso, boys, Renso.)
Still he shipped on a Yankee whaler,
 (Renso, boys, Renso)
He could not do his duty,
 (Renso, boys, Renso.)
And he tried to run away then,
 (Renso, boys, Renso.)
They caught and brought him back again,
 (Renso, boys, Renso.)
And he said he never would go again,
 (Renso, boys, Renso.)
They put him pounding cable,
 (Renso, boys, Renso.)
And found him very able,
 (Renso, boys, Renso.)
He said he'd run away no more,
 (Renso, boys, Renso.)
He only waited to get on shore,
 (Renso, boys, Renso.)
So when he put his feet on shore,
 (Renso, boys, Renso.)
A-whaling he would go no more,
 (Renso, boys, Renso.)"

What a whale that was! He was the biggest fellow I ever fell in with. He measured sixty-four feet over all, and he had a sixteen-foot jaw. His flukes stretched sixteen feet from tip to tip. He made a hundred and thirty barrels of oil.

"Think what that old spouter must have weighed," said the mate, when we had got him coopered. "One hundred and thirty barrels at eight pounds a gallon — that makes — let me see — that makes" (scratching of head, squirming of eyebrows, smile of relief at last) "that makes two thousand, seven hundred and sixty pounds of oil."

"Here, here!" I said, "work that out on paper, Mr. Wilson; let's be accurate. I'd really like to get at the facts."

So Mr. Dorman figured it out in unimpeachable black and white. He was right. Two thousand, seven hundred and sixty pounds of oil!

"Now, Cap'n Robbins," he continued, "you'll grant it's within limits to say, one-third oil, two-thirds waste?"

"Yes, a fair estimate; nobody can dispute that."

"Now, then," bending over the black and white and cautiously plying the pencil, "three-times – aught – is – aught – three – times – six – is – eight and–one–to–carry–three – times–seven–is–one–and one–to–carry–is–two – and – two – to – carry–three times–two — — — — — — — — — — — — — There! Eight thousand, two hundred and eighty pounds. Great Cæsar!"

THE GAM.

"I'd ruther gam for fifteen minutes than slush the mast for fifteen weeks."
—*Rubaiyat of Salthorse Dooley.*

"WHAT did you say your old man's name was?"

" Robbins, shipmates, an' as thorough a seaman as ever trod the quarter-deck."

" Strict ?"

" Yes — an' no. You don't feel like you was being governed, an' yit ev'ry man aboard done what he said, ev'ry time. They ain't no half-laughs an' sailor's grins about him. He's straight up an' down, like a yard o' pump water ! "

" A jolly wag, too!" broke in a third heavy voice. " You ought to seen him play it on them full-rig Mohammedans at Johanna. By George, it was fun ! Worth a man's hull advance pay!"

Two bells ! One o'clock in the morning ! And the ships were gamming still. The two captains were holding high converse in the *Clara Bell's* cabin, and until the visiting master saw fit to return to his vessel, the visiting watch from the stranger made merry in the *Clara Bell's* fore-castle. It was a delight to see new faces. It was a rare treat to hear new voices. It was a fine, novel pleasure to match yarns all round.

The men sat on the stout sea-chests along the sides of that semi-circular room in the whale-ship's bow. There were eighteen men in all; nine were hosts, nine were guests. Light streamed down upon them from greasy lamps hung up on the bitts. The air was dim with the smoke of cheap tobacco.

Gamming is distinctly a whaleman's pastime. Merchant ships will pass each other in mid-ocean without a sign of recognition, steam-craft will go by with a snobbish air that almost approaches hostility, but whale-ships, when they meet, are friendlier. They will heave to, after the day's cruising is over and there is no longer any chance of raising whales, and the captain's watch of one ship will entertain the captain's watch of the other ship. Similarly, the two chief mates' watches come together. This is called "gamming."

On that particular occasion the *Clara Bell's* forecastle had been a hilarious roistering place since seven in the evening. There had been songs and cards and smoke; and smoke and cards and songs. There had been long-spun, hair-lifting narratives of whaling adventures. There had also been news from home — some of it a year old, but still very startling; and some of it six months new, every word an eye-opener.

And now they had taken to telling land-yarns and stories of recent ports. Plainly, the gam was about gammed out.

" Well, chummy, what about Johanna ? "

" Dy'e know the place ? "

" Know it ? Guess I do. Here's my tarry flipper on it! Know Johanny, do I ? I knowed Johanny 'fore I'd learnt my three L's. It's got high hills 'round it, an' you can see 'em forty mile out to sea, — ain't I right ? An' them white stone houses in the town — they ain't no taller, b'gosh, than a whaleship's hurricane house. Ain't that so, messmate ? An' them copper-colored natives, an' their gaff-tops'l turbans, an' their white gowns as if they was goin' to be buried at sea, an' the beetle-nut they chews that gits their teeth as black as tar an' gits the deck as red as blood, b'gosh, so nothin' short o' the prayer-books 'll take it off ag'in, — don't I remember 'em ? Who says I ain't been to Johanny ? "

But the third voice, who seemed to think himself particularly predestined and foreordained to man the pumps and keep the stories flowing, urged again, " What about the old man and the natives ? Tell us, chummy. "

So " Bilge " Dennett took his pipe out of his broad mouth, and tapping the bowl gently against the sea-chest, dumped the ashes on the forecastle floor.

"Well, boys," he said, looking out craftily from under his ragged red eye-brows and lifting an awkward forefinger in a jerky gesture, as if to say, "Keep your weather eye open; she's coming!" — "Well, boys; you know how them sogerin' Moslems hates pork, 'an pork-grease, an any sort o' grease. Worse 'n Sheenies, ain't they?

"Well, the old man, he comes it on 'em mighty ship-shape. He'd clap a lump o' butter in the palm o' his flipper just 'fore he come up on deck in the morin'; an pretty soon a brown Ay–rab would sail up to him to talk tradin' 'an that like; an' when them two spliced hands it was worse 'n whales an' killers.

"Then, by the bloody wars, they was a tornado! That Moslem would be brought up all standin', an' he'd jump back an' pull his sheath-knife out o' his belt and strike a figger like a villian in a play, an' sing out, 'If you wa' n't my friend, I'd kill you in a minute!' You ought to see it, lads.

"Then the old man would sing out for the cabin-boy to turn to an' fetch a basin o' water an' a clean towel, an' when the Ay–rab had swabbed his flipper he'd feel chummy again and then them

10

two would love each other just like nothin'
oncommon 'd happened."

An appreciative grin spread over the faces of
the listeners.

"Just wait till *we* put in at Johanna," said
one; "we'll butter them natives; we'll make
buttered rolls of the whole crew of 'em; *blowed*
if we wont."

Then Bilge resumed.

"That ain't the only thing the old man done at
Johanna, bless his old soul. One day he goes on
shore an' cruises 'round with a Moslem merchant
intendin' to go to the brown man's house. All on
a sudden a bell rings out from a big white mosque,
an' down drops the brown man on his knees like
he was shot — down killick! — an' he clapped his
head three times on the ground an' had over a
long pious chanty in Ay-rab lingo, an' then up he
got ag'in an' looked 'round for the old man. But
the old man, bless his soul, he'd forged ahead
while the brown man was hove down, an' so he
come up to the house first. Ha, ha!

"Now you know how shy them Johanna
women be."

"Guess I do," broke in the Man Who Had
Been There Himself. "You *bet* I do! You can
gamble on that, night an' day, b'gosh! You cruise

around them crooked streets, lookin', an lookin', an' lookin', but b'gosh you don't raise a gal! Them women gits from house to house by goin' aloft an' sneaking' along them flat roofs, b'gosh! An' a chap don't see his Nancy till they're spliced in the mosque by some sky-pilot or Holy Joe or other, or whatever them Ay–rabs calls him!"

"Aye-aye, messmate, we all know you've been there, but Bilge Dennett is holding the yarn. You ain't. Go on, Bilgy! What did the old man do when he dropped his mud-hook in the Ay–rab's shanty?" The speaker was one of the visiting watch. The Man Who Had Been There Himself subsided.

"Well," Bilgy resumed, relieved at being no longer interrupted, "'taint so much what he done inside as what he never done at all when he first cume up to the door. They's a kind o' harbor law to Johanna it says you must give three loud raps on the door an' a good waitin' spell 'tween the raps so's to let the women folks know a man's a-comin' an' put for shelter. That's the rule o' the road an' there's the devil to pay if you don't sail by it.

"Well, the old man, bless his jolly toplights, he just give the door one good thump an' then in he forged all ataunto.

" There in the cabin — I mean, there in the parlor, — was the Ay-rab's wife and daughter, with not more'n half their standin' riggin' on, naked from their waists up! Heavens, wa'n't they gallied! They jumped for safety like a brace o' jack-rabbits.

" Then that Ay-rab begun cussin' worse'n forty pirates on a raft! Thunder an' lightnin', but didn't he give it to the old man! but the old man just keeps a' talkin' business — so many fathom o' cotton cloth for so many live hogs, so many pounds o' gunpowder for so many cords o' wood, an' so on an' so on — till at last the brown man cools off as cool as a cask o' sperm oil all fit to be coopered.

" An frien's an' fellow cit'zens, as they say in town-meetin' back in old Vermont, that's how I have the honor (a-hem) to be sailin' under the only live Yankee that ever saw a woman in Johanna."

There was an evident demand for Johanna stories. The *Clara Bell's* men liked to hear the captain's prowess enlarged upon. The strangers liked to learn all they could about Johanna so as not to be altogether green when they came into port, and every Jack Tar of them was vowing in his innermost heart of hearts and swearing by all

that's ship-shape that *he'd* make those Arabs dance
a break-down and teach them just a few new steps
into the bargain.

" Come, Bilgy, my jolly sea-dog, tell 'em about
the coffee. *That'll* start their stanchions!' "

" Yes, Bilgy, tell 'em how the steward hazed
them Ay–rab waisters !' "

" Aye-aye, Bilgy, clew up your jawin' tackle,
an' you'll make these here jolly strangers grin
like so many right whales !' "

" Come, tumble up, my lively hearty, out with
the twister!' "

" On one condition an' one only," said Bilge
Dennett, " an' that condition is this, mess-mates:
I'll spin the yarn, but only after that there man-
o'-war's-man's sung us another rare old chanty.
So, Four-decker, give us a broadside ! Can't you
bellow the ' Commodore ', or have you clean forgot
it, so long since you was a blue-jacket?' "

" The ' Commodore ' — give us the ' Commodore,' " the sailors shouted, "give us the ' Commodore ', or we'll scuttle your old hulk and send you
plumb to Jimmy Squarefoot."

The blue-jacket — or, as some would say, the
jolly — was proud of his former service in the
navy, so proud, in fact, that he thought he had
stepped down a ratline or two in reducing himself

to a mere mercenary blubber-hunter. He had been waiting all the evening for somebody to call for a line-of-battle-ship yarn, but this invitation to sing was the nearest approach to such solicitation. He therefore jumped at the chance. He assumed for the moment an air of aggrieved timidity, but when the crowd insisted, he reluctantly, but firmly, submitted.

Four-decker was a stout, deep-chested, beef-laden seaman with a cavernous mouth and a ponderous bass voice. He sang with the gusto of a music-hall soloist and an occasional tragic gesture enlivened the ballad : —

> " It was on a dark and stormy night,
>   The wind nor'west did blow;
>   And from the ship's high, lofty bows,
>   That were pitching to and fro,
>   Could be heard loud, rattling peals of thunder,
>   And fierce, wild lightnings fly.
>   Hail, rain and sleet and thunders meet,
>   And dismal was the sky.

> " 'Twas early on next morning
>   Our brave commander said
> ' Whoever has the lookout, go up to the mast-head,
>   And keep a good lookout, my boy,
>   And try what you can see! '
>   And he soon cried out from the mast-head,
> ' Two large ships under our lee! '

> " Now one was off our quarter,
>   The other off our cat-head.
>   We cleared away for action,
>   As our brave commander said.

The job being done. it counted one,
And lasted from twelve till four,
And what was fearful to relate,
We sank the French *Commodore!*

' Now five sailors we picked up were Frenchmen,
And six were from haughty Spain.
We picked them up from off the wreck,
That had floated from the main.
Soon we'll send them to proud France,
Where they had been before,
To tell the proud French admiral
We sank his *Commodore.*"

The singer wound up his song with a lusty
cadenza that made the forecastle fairly shiver
with its vibrant, tragic resonance. It was easy
to see that Four-decker considered himself entirely
responsible for the sinking of the *Commodore.*
You would have thought it his habit, had you
heard him sing, to engage a foreign corvette or
sloop-of-war every ten or fifteen minutes.

There was a hearty round of applause, much
kicking of heels against sea-chests and a prodigious clapping of hardened hards, but no verbal
suggestion of an encore. A whaleman never dips
his colors to man-of-war service.

It was a trying moment, but Four-decker was
quick to see the dignified way of escape out of
his embarrassment.

" Now, Bilge," he said, with an assumption of
fervent enthusiasm, "it's *your* trick at the wheel!"

" Yes, Bilge," shouted the Social Pump, " tell 'em about that ' much-good ' coffee."

" Well, boys," Bilge Dennet resumed, " we get bully good coffee aboard o' this here barkie, an' you can bet your spare yards on that. An' when them Ay-rabs come on board to trade, the steward, bless his soul, he'd lure the whole school of 'em into the cabin an' treat 'em to hot coffee all round. An' that jolly flunky knows how to mix the drink so it'll lift your hair like a flaw o' wind. It's the real thing — none o' your water-bewitched, *I* tell you ! "

" Kind o' lives up to the rule they have in Ryo Janeero, I reckon," added the Experienced Man, parenthetically. " Jolly good rule, too, b'gosh ! "

" What's that ? " queried Bilge Dennett.

" Why, them yellow-belly Portugees say, ' Coffee, to be A1, must be black as night, strong as death, an' hot as hell !' — that's the rule, b'gosh, an' you can bet your rudder them Dagoes lives up to it ! "

" Ay   aye," said Bilge, " that's the chart our flunky sails by, bless his tarry soul, an' he never let's the doctor touch the mixture when he wants to come out extra man-o'-war-fashion. An' as I was sayin', mess-mates, them turban Ay–rabs took to it like whales take to water.

"'Much good, much good!' they'd say an' hold out their cups for more.

"Well, this sort o' thing made the steward mighty popular, *I* tell you; he could 'a' been king o' the island any time he'd say the word; but that everlastin' coffee cookin' got to be a pesky nuisance, an' at last the flunky hit on a trick to chop it off square.

"So one day he hailed them traders an' says to 'em, 'Come down in the cabin, gents. an' splice the main-brace with a cup of **A1** coffee!'

"So down they climbs, every brown Alladin's son of 'em, an' that cabin was as full of Ay–rabs as the hold was full of casks. An' then the flunky serves out that coffee, made a-purpose, bless his spankin' soul,— black an' hot an' strong — till it lifted their turbans for 'em boys, an' made 'em wiggle in their chairs. 'Much good, much good, much good!' they yelled, an' the flunkey kep' a-pourin' an' a-pourin' till he'd emptied the whole blessed pot.

"'Well, gents', he says, 'did you ever swaller such coffee, in all your heathen born days? Come, gents, *did* you?' an' them **Ay**–rabs says, 'No, most honorable, we never done it.'

"An' then, boys, what do you think? That flunky runs a fork down in the coffee pot, and claws 'round in them black grounds, an' fishes out a long bit o' salt pork rind, an' holds it up front o' their crazy top-lights.

"Then you ought to seen the hurricane. That shiny pork knocked them Ay-rabs alow an' aloft. They was hit with the horrors. Their head-lights stuck out so you could hang your hat on 'em. They turned from brown to white.

"An' afore you could sing the first line of 'Jack Robinson' the whole school of 'em tumbled up like the watch below when 'all hands' is called. Out them Ay-rabs bounced — oh, boys, it was worth a bottle o' close-reef to see 'em! They scudded for the ship's side like a dozen white yachts in a gale, and there they tickled their hot-copper gullets with their finger-ends so as to git clear o' that 'much good' coffee! An' mateys, that ended the coffee nuisance for good an' all, *I* tell you."

No sooner was the story finished than there was a prodigious banging on the forecastle scuttle, followed by a sharp call of command. The stranger crew were summoned on deck to return to their ship, and the gam was over.

I have ever since pitied the Moslems of Johanna for the treatment they must have got from the whalemen who were so elaborately coached, that night, in the *Clara Bell's* forecastle.

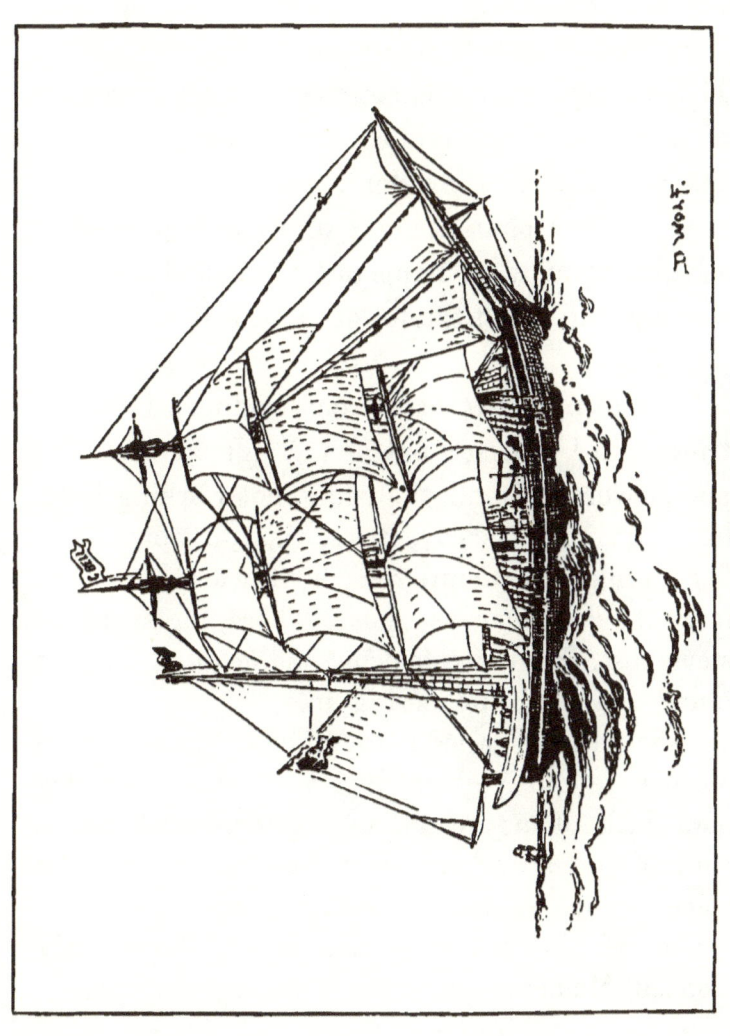

THE BARK "CLARA BELL."

AUGUSTINE BAY.

NOT a story this time. Instead, a string of stories. For things come about at sea, as upon land, without much reference to literary values. They simply occur. Sometimes they are dramatic; oftener not. Sometimes they steer towards a climax; oftener they don't.

So this is a plain account of what happened — an account of what happened to me and my crew and my ship when the lot of us called at Augustine Bay.

The *Clara Bell* had been leaking. It was a trifle, said I at first; but now it got worse. The pumps were at it all the while, not working hard, but working. Clearly, it was time to worry.

Searching the damp, dark hold, we made out at last the treacherous spot. There, against the stern-post, about two feet below the water-line, we found the sea-brine oozing in.

I should have called it tough luck, this wretched obstacle to our voyage, had we not been every man Jack of us ready to welcome such interruption. For our cruise was up. Port was the place for us, so we put away.

Out of the sea rose the green, luxuriantly wooded Madagascan coast, — within the coast a

lovely harbor, the harbor of Augustine Bay.
Entering there, we dropped our mudhook off
Tent Rock. Very well named, I call that rock,
for it is shaped like a tent and as white as new
canvas. It is just a mile from the shore.

I can't say how it is now, but in those old days
whoever bethought him to land at Augustine Bay
must first make terms with the savages. I knew
that the fuzzy fellows would soon come off to treat
with us. Accordingly I cleared for action. For
savages are thieves, the whole world over, and
whatever may be said in favor of valor, discretion is the better part of holding your own.
Every dispensable article went below — rope,
spare belaying-pins, buckets, craft — lest those
rogues should make off with them.

Now I confess to a weakness for dogs, particularly for big Newfoundland dogs, and most
particularly for my beloved black Rover. I was
bound that no sooty Madagascan should capture
that faithful friend. I therefore shut Rover up.
I tucked him into my room off the cabin and left
him there for safe keeping.

And in that I builded better than I knew.

Hardly had I got upon deck again when the
canoes, deeply laden with their savage freight,
came splashing for us. Then there was a wild

scramble up the ship's side. The natives climbed
up over the bulwarks like ants out of a broken
hill. They were terrible fellows. They had grass
mats around their loins. Some had arrayed themselves in dirty flannel shirts. Their women wore
nondescript garments of cotton cloth, and had
their hair done up in little knots like nutmegs
and covered with grease.

We set to business directly. The chief and his
cabinet — "big men," they say — followed me
down into the cabin, where the pow-wow began.
I wanted to land and to recruit the *Clara Bell*
with wood and water. I wanted to buy that
privilege cheap. They, on their part, wanted
cotton cloth. They wanted all they could get
of it. And that's where we disagreed.

Whatever those fuzzies thought of my seaman-
ship, they evidently held a very low estimate of
my diplomacy ; but in that they were mistaken.
For we had gammed with a ship from that very
port and I knew the ropes like any old sea-dog.
I knew just how much I ought to give, and just
where I ought to draw the line. The regulation
tariff was thirty yards to the chief and five
fathoms to each of his advisers. That I offered
and there I stuck.

But time was precious and I knew that, too.
For I had two tribes to deal with. These chaps

at Tent Rock could not give me leave to get water at the head of the river. Another tribe from that quarter would come along directly and I must get rid of present company before that. But how the rascals hung on! They haggled over prices hour after hour. They were like a batch of Soloman Levis. Indeed, I believe they were descended from the long-lost tribes of Israel.

I was pretty well driven to destraction, when suddenly Rover burst the bonds of his imprisonment.

Out he bounded into the cabin and then — oh, lands and seas, how those chumps did scoot! They had never seen a dog before! They jumped out of that cabin like electrified jack-rabbits. Rover followed hard and the whole tribe, save only the chief, made off over the ship's bows, each one taking the cloth he had held at the moment of Rover's appearance — some content with only a fathom, others counting themselves lucky with a strip three yards long.

As for the chief, his knees were knocking together and his eyes were starting from their sockets. He made terms in a hurry.

But when the up-river folk came off, I had to be generous. I wanted to tow our raft of casks a long way up their river to get fresh water, and I

was aware that we should have to wait over night
before we could bring them back to the ship. We
must make fast friends with the natives or they
would steal the hoops off our casks and then, so
far as practical purposes went, there wouldn't be
any casks.

We made ourselves "solid" with both chiefs,
and according to agreement they left a native
detective on board to make sure we were not
troubled with thieving. Little good came of that,
however, for the detective was the worst thief of
the lot. That, please observe, is saying a great
deal. The gift for misappropriation is nowhere
more superbly developed than in Madagascar.
And their impudence, combined with their thieving — pity the mariner who must restrain himself
from bloodshed under such torment! No sort of
sanctity is proof against their ravages.

One day a Yankee clipper came to anchor in
the harbor with the stars and stripes at her peak.

While the captain and his officers were at supper, the fuzzies hauled down Old Glory and made
off with it. The Tent Rock chief, so I have
heard, had it made up into a suit of clothes, and
was seen by a British crew, a few weeks later,
strutting about in it like a coal-tar Yankee Doodle.
But all that happened after we had left.

Often, while we lay in port, the up-river chief and his dusky queen and their suite came off to visit us. We counted that no serious affliction, for in Madagascar you can entertain royalty on a very slender outlay. We would put a huge wash-tub on the quarter deck, pour two or three pails of water into it, sweeten the water with a quart of molasses, and add ten or a dozen pounds of ship's biscuit. The royal cortege would squat round the tub — a guzzling, grinning, jabbering ring of boobies — thinking themselves lavishly entertained.

Big fun we called that. But that was not our only sport at Augustine Bay. In fact it was as nothing beside our mischievous practice of medicine.

One day a native came aboard clutching his aching belly, and groaning in misery. I knew what he wanted, and gave him a nip of New England rum. Instantaneous cure!

Next day, however, Mr. Fuzzy came back for further treatment. His case was serious. He said he had been ill for a year. One dose was not enough to eradicate a chronic disorder. Of course not, who ever said it was?

I therefore turned my patient over to the mate, who saw a chance to make something out of the

11

Fuzzy's weakness. The two hit on a capital agreement — the Fuzzy to bring a bucket of beans on board every day, the mate to "cure" the Fuzzy.

Now that mate of mine had ideas of his own, and this is the series of doses he gave that poor heathen : —

First day,— half-glass of rum and four table-spoonfuls castor oil.

Second day,— hot-drops, sugar and water.

Third-day,— vinegar and pepper-sauce.

Fourth day,— molasses and mustard.

Fifth day,— glass of brandy with red pepper.

Sixth day,— cayenne pepper and cheese.

Seventh day — onions, mustard and Chili sauce.

Eighth day,— rum and castor oil, same as first day.

Ninth day — arnica, paregoric and mustard, equal parts.

Tenth day,— straight whiskey.

With what result? The very best, the very best result in the world. The black beggar stuck it out bravely, patient to the bitter end. He would take his medicine with utter resignation. He would twist his coarse face into hideous grimaces. He would go away feeling as if he had swallowed a bonfire. But when the time expired he was thoroughly cured. As is commonly the case, he got well in spite of his medicine!

Of course we had the usual port routine to follow up. Beside water and wood, we laid in a supply of beans — much like Lima beans, and a lot of beef and mutton. The live beef was a sight. The bullocks were large and fat, with humps on their fore-shoulders. Splendid fellows they were, sleek as silk, the finest I ever saw! And the prices! — you could buy them for an old flint-lock musket and a few brass-headed tacks. (Why the tacks? you ask. For ornament. The savages pound them into the wooden parts of their guns.) We would purchase those bullocks on the shore and then we would swim them off to the ship and hoist them in by their long horns.

Then, too, there was the matter of the leak. That had to be attended to immediately. We took the cargo out of the after part of the ship to lighten her, and then we found the cause of the trouble.

There are no accidents in the world — never were — never will be. Everything has its cause, and that particular thing, the leak, had this cause — the copper bottom had not been securely soldered about the stern-post. Through the tiny water-course thus left exposed, the worms had got in — puny creatures, so small you could hardly see them with the naked eye, yet they had bored those solid white-oak planks into a sieve like a honey-comb. A blow from a hammer on the worm-eaten parts would crush the wood in like an egg shell. There was a weak spot, easily repaired, that might have sent us to Davy Jones.

Before we left Augustine Bay, a fine clipper swept up the harbor and anchored near us, the French tri-color at her peak. According to the best accounts, she had come into port to procure a cargo of laborers. Innocent word enough, — laborers! Ah, but she would take them to the island of Bourbon. There they would be paid twelve dollars a month for seven years' service.

And what of that? Just this : they would never be able to buy their way out of bondage. The seven years up, they would all be in debt and would have to remain as slaves, powerless even to return home. It was slavery in disguise.

Out of the remote interior of the island came that sombre procession. A slave trader had them in leash. He herded them all the way to the shore, and he himself brought them, load after load, aboard the French ship. Once on deck the poor creatures were examined by a sort of veterinary, who punched their breasts, pinched their limbs and eyed their teeth as if he were appraising so much horseflesh. Oh, it was a horrid sight! And I saw it done.

In the midst of the operation a man-of-war, cruising for slavers, entered the harbor. A boat sped swiftly across the water, and the officers boarded the Frenchman. But nothing could be contrived to save the poor wretches. The Frenchman's papers were flawless. Dastardly though the fact, it was cloaked in a legal fiction. No one had a right to interfere.

The process of examination went steadily forward. The young and strong were taken. The old and decrepit were rejected. Lucky, indeed, were the physically unfit.

When our repairs were done and all supplies got in and stowed down, we took our mudhook and put to sea, beating out of Augustine Bay in the early afternoon.

Down into the southern sea sank those pleasant shores, slowly and almost reluctantly, but bold against the far horizon we could still see the ugly form of the slaver, swift upon her way toward Bourbon.

THE ALBATROSS.

" God save thee, Ancient Mariner,
    From the fiends that plague thee thus!
Why looks thou so? With my cross-bow
I shot the Albatross."

— *Coleridge.*

" Cap'n Robbins, I beg you, don't ! "

" Don't — ? "

" Don't kill the albatross."

" And, pray, why shouldn't I ? "

" Because," said the mate of the *Thomas Pope*, " it's well known, sir, that terrible consequences follow the murder of one of those white birds. I say *murder* — for I can tell you, sir, it's nothing less. Haven't you heard that the souls of dead bo's'ns and sailors go soaring about in these latitudes in the form of albatrosses ? "

" Why, no," I answered, " You see I never lived in the fo'c's'le, Mr. Russell. My first voyage I shipped as cabin-boy, and my second voyage I went as third mate in the old *Balaena*. So, you see, I never got much acquainted with the fo'c's'le superstitions."

" What ! " Russell exclaimed, " has no one ever told you how dangerous it is to kill an albatross ? "

Preparations for albatross-catching were already going bravely forward in the waist. The sailors were busy rigging a long, stout fish-line with a big cod-hook at the end. They were getting a liberal slice of salt-pork to bait the hook. That never fails.

"Well," said my mate, "I notice that my opinions don't weigh any too heavy with you; but tell me, sir, have you ever killed an albatross before?"

"Lots of them. Last time I was rounding the Cape of Good Hope I killed half-a-dozen. Why, if I'm not mistaken, it was only a few sea-miles from where we are just now."

"And no unpleasant consequence followed?"

"Oh, well, to be frank with you, I *did* come near losing my ship within a few days after that."

"See," said Russell, "see how that bird hovers over the main-mast truck! The creature must measure at least ten feet across those wings! And think of it, sir, the albatross has followed us for three days now — or is it four? But pardon the interruption — what was that about all but losing your ship?"

"Why, it was on one of my voyages homeward from the Indian Ocean. We were lying to in a gale. And all of a sudden the wind changed and brought us into the trough of the sea, so that we were forced to wear ship to keep our decks from being swept of everything and losing our boats. 'Meet her when she shakes,' the mate shouted, 'full for stays!' But when the wheel was put up, and the ship had gathered headway, a great, rolling swell caught her bodily, and turned her over on her beam-ends. There we lay, apparently undecided which way to go, trucks up or keel up. I lived twenty years in twenty seconds! Then the awful moments of suspense went by. The ship righted herself angrily — mad as a whale in his flurry — and we came round breasting the sea!"

"A marvellous escape!" Russell observed, with the air of a mathematician about to say Q. E. D.

"Yes, a marvellous escape! Many a good stanch hooker has gone to Davy Jones just that way. I was lucky to have a long-legged ship. If she had been one of those round-ribbed, flat-bottomed butter-boxes they build by the mile down in Maine and saw off any length you order, we should surely have turned turtle and never been heard from again!"

"Aha!" said Russell, with a twinkle of triumph in his little black eyes, "Seems to me your own experience confirms the truth of my convictions!"

" O, not at all!" I answered. " If my logic
serves me well, all it proves is that when you get
into a mighty bad scrape you get out of it unhurt.
If killing albatrosses has anything to do with that,
why, where's the harm of killing them? It
strikes me, Mr. Russell, we'd better take special
pains to kill a few birds, you and I, (or murder,
them, if you prefer), as a precautionary measure!
At any rate, we'll have that big bird yonder, I
reckon, the very next swoop he makes. These
bo's'ns' ghosts of yours don't show any very
dainty taste in the bait they snap at — eh, Mr.
Russell?"

Russell was about to venture a reply, when
suddenly, just as I had predicted, the albatross
swooped down upon that irresistible bait of salt
pork. The hook took a cruel hold in the big
fowl's throat. The line was stretched taut. You
would have thought the bird would break his long
swan-neck, he struggled so madly to be free.
Four men held the line; they hauled it in; they
grappled with the albatross and they killed him.

The mate stood horrified. His hands were
thrust deep in the pockets of his blue roundabout; they twitched nervously. His mouth
tightened at the corners and made deep wrinkles
in his yellow cheeks. He turned to me with a

look of outraged anxiety and spoke tremulously, "Cap'n Robbins," he said, "we shall all be very sorry for this — very, very sorry, and that not many days from now!"

"As for the truth of that cheerful prophecy," I answered, "it's more a matter of fact than of opinion. Let us wait and see!" pleasantly enough I smiled as I spoke, but Russell's frown grew only the gloomier.

The albatross found his way in time into the cook's coppers and thence at dinner-hour, albeit a trifle tardy, into the cabin. He was served in a delicious sea-pie, though my wife, who was then upon her first voyage, and by no means the tall-water epicure she afterward became, pronounced him decidedly strong and fishy.

I watched the mate closely, not a little curious to see how he would behave. He was ashamed not to take his portion of that double-decker pie upon his plate, but I noticed that he contented himself with nibbling the potatoes and onions that went with the meat, while of the meat itself he never tasted the tinest morsel. His objections, forsooth, were conscientious. He was not going to incur the guilt of cannibalism.

"Russell," I said, "we were speaking of the possible consequences of killing an albatross, you

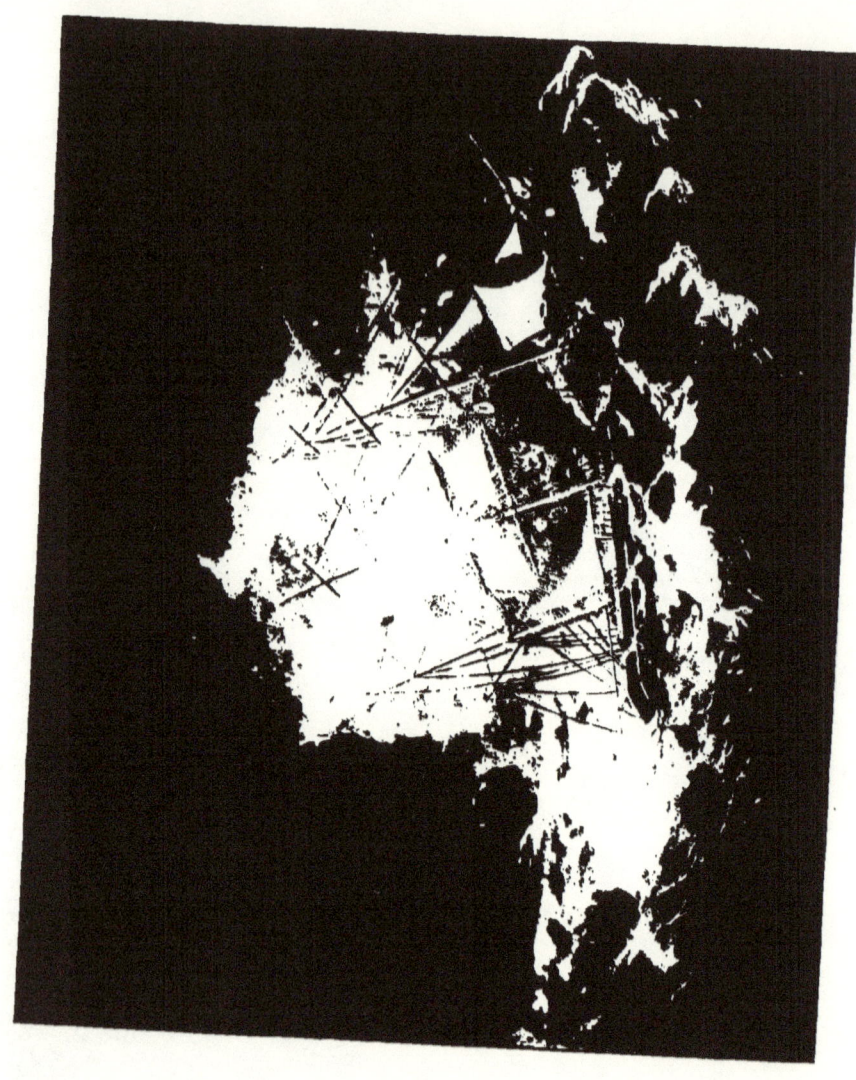

ST. ELMO'S FIRE.

remember, and I told you this morning that I had only one experience to judge by. That is hardly true. There was another occasion I ought to have mentioned."

" And that was ?——"

" A most extraordinary occurence, Mr. Russell. I was coming home from one of my merchant voyages. The ship was nearing the Gulf Stream on her course from Pernambuco. A heavy sou'-west gale was blowing, and the old girl was running under close-reefed main-top-sail and fore-sail.

"We entered the Gulf Stream about midnight. The wind died out to a calm. Heavy, oily, black clouds piled up in the nor'-east and covered the sky till it was dark as the ship's run. I thought the wind would come from that direction and strike the ship aback, so I called all hands to take in main-top-s'l and fore-s'l. You know merchant ships go with such stingy crews it leaves you short-handed at a time like that. Consequently I had to take the wheel.

"The men had got hold of the clew-lines and bunt-lines, and were about to start the sheets, when there was a sudden flash in the sou'-west and a ball of blazing fire as big as a man's head leaped out of the clouds. It dashed across the

sky. It made for our ship. It started at an angle
of forty-five degrees, and it modified its course
into a curving line like part of an ellipse. A
trail of fire followed it. It struck the main-top-
m'st just above the cap on the head of the
main-m'st and exploded with a report like that of
a rifle. The sparks flew into the belly of the
main-top-s'l. The light blinded my eyes.

"As soon as I could see again, I looked for my
men. They had all tumbled out of sight. I
locked the wheel and went for'ard. There I
found the crew lying on the deck in the ship's
waist — senseless every man Jack of them. After
a few minutes they all came to but one. He was
a young Portuguese. We carried him down into
the cabin and rubbed him and dosed him and put
smelling-salts under his nose, and at last he
opened his eyes and said, '*Bono Dio*, Cap, I don't
want see all-same-that again!'

"In the morning I examined the mast with the
utmost care, but I could find nowhere any mark
left by that flying ball of flame. The thing was
evidently a sort of 'St. Elmo's Fire'; but you
may imagine my horror when I found my crew
all unconscious. Heavens! I thought for a
moment that I was the only live man left aboard
that ship!"

"Yes," said Russell, "I have read of such things, and I knew a man once who had seen one. He called it a corposant — or compresent, some say; but what puzzles me, Cap'n Robbins, is to see what sort of connection there is between a ball of electric fire in the Gulf Stream and the killing of an albatross. I never heard of albatrosses in those latitudes, did you, sir?"

"No, hardly," I answered, "but since you've begun to enlighten me, I am inclined to attribute that occurrence to an albatross I had 'murdered' three years before!"

Russell munched his onions and potatoes in silence. I hope he enjoyed them. The conversation lapsed; the meal was nearly done before it revived again.

The next day, — according to my log-book it was the twentieth of November, back in fifty-nine, — we were struck by a furious gale, the first real storm since the voyage began. Our little bark scudded under close-reefed main-top-sail and fore-sail before a fierce sou'west wind. Albatross or no albatross, it was blowing great guns. The ship labored frightfully. The green hand at the helm would let her come to a little now and then, and every time he did it, she would take a sea in the waist with a noise like thunder. I had to watch him as you watch a madman.

At seven bells that morning, the steward had got the racks on the table, and was putting our breakfast in readiness. I was below at the moment. The ship was pitching and heaving till I thought she would jump the sticks out of her. Suddenly she brought a tremendous roll to starboard. I shouted to the cabin-boy, "Look out for the table!" but the words were no more than spoken when everything slid off on to the floor with forty different kinds of jingles and crashes all at once. My wife shicked with terror; she thought we were wrecked; she rushed from the state-room in her night-gown, and just at that moment a monstrous wave pooped the *Thomas Pope*, and burst over the ship's port quarter. Tons of salt water came pounding through the sky-light into the after-cabin, and Mrs. Robbins arrived upon the scene at the one happy moment when she would get the full benefit of it. That sea-going wife of mine has no taste for immersion; but on that memorable morning she could not choose but submit. As I said at the time, that big, cold billow baptized her for the Indian Ocean.

I was glad, a few days later, that it had done so, for after so tremendous an initiation she never

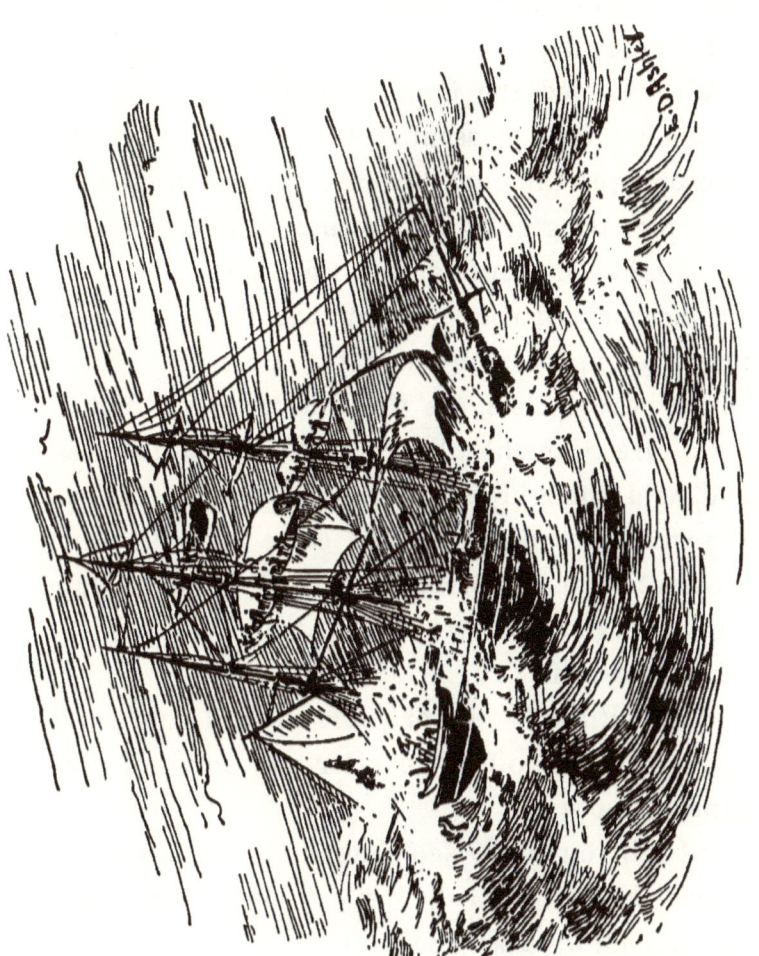

ROUNDING CAPE OF GOOD HOPE.

again suffered any fear. I think she regarded herself as one who had endured the worst there was to endure, and resolved not to be annoyed by trifles thereafter.

We rounded the Cape, and then the weather became more pleasant. We steered for the Mozambique Channel, keeping the watch on deck busy preparing craft and cutting-gear for whaling. We might see whales at any time now.

Since that roaring gale off the Cape, the chief mate had never mentioned the albatross. But I could, nevertheless, see that his mind was not at rest. He thought albatross, dreamed albatross, and, as I thought, even looked albatross. When the weather moderated and came off warm and pleasant with favorable winds, I watched him with a curious interest. A last I broached the matter myself.

"Mr. Russell," I said, "it strikes me we're going to come off alive after all, spite of that cannibal pot-pie!"

"I tell you what, Cap'n Robbins," he answered, unmistakably nettled, "we're not home yet! No, sir, *not by a long sea mile!*"

No sooner had he spoken those ominous words than I observed a hugh rolling swell, miles in extent, and straight as the spanker-boom, coming down upon us from the north'ard. The wind had died out to a flat calm. There was not a ripple of white water under the ship's fore-foot. There was not a streak of foam nor so much as a bubble in her wake. It was an Irishman's tempest, straight up and down! The air was hazy, sultry, and almost unbearably hot. There could then be but one meaning in the powerful swell that bore down upon the *Thomas Pope*. To the northward, just beyond that peaceful horizon, a hurricane was raging. The roller had been sent out by it.

A ripple rushes out from a stone dropped in a mill-pond. That roller was the ripple magnified to sublime proportions.

Another roller — another! Then, quicker than the first three, still another! And as yet no faintest flaw of wind!

We were trapped. The albatross would be avenged, and Russell vindicated.

We were then about in the middle of Mozambique Channel. Madagascar was some three hundred miles to the eastward, and the coast of Africa about the same distance off in the opposite direction.

For a day and a night the flat calm continued. Then a light breeze sprang up from the sou'east.

"THOMAS POPE" BEFORE THE STORM.

All the afternoon the wind increased, first gradually, then rapidly, so rapidly that at sundown we
had the *Pope* under storm canvas — close-reefed
top-sails and reefed foresail. The wind kept fresh-
ening. It veered steadily toward the east. It
raged with increasing fury, a fresh hand at the
bellows. The ship was talking loudly — pitching
and pounding — bobbing at it with a will. At ten
o'clock it was blowing a furious gale. We had
got in all sail, save close-reef main-top-sail and
reefed fore-sail. At mid-night matters grew worse.
We got the *Pope* under main-spencer and fore-
top-mast-stay-sail. The wind was blowing with
maddened frenzy. The ship was over on her
beam ends, with larboard rails and three boats
under water.

I called all hands to batten down the hatches.
We stretched the tarpaulins tight across them and
we nailed the battens fast to the coamings and
head-ledges.

By two o'clock in the morning the spencers
and fore-top-mast stay-sails had blown away. The
sails on the yards were working loose from under
the gaskets. I sent men into the rigging to
secure them, but they could not get aloft. When
they were about ten feet up, the wind pinned
them tight against the ratlines. They were like

dead men. I shouted to them to come back, but the wind carried the sound away. You could not have made them hear with a trumpet. I waved my arms at them and they struggled down on deck and made their way aft with ducked heads, coming hand over hand, clinging to the belaying pins along the starboard bulwarks.

The storm had its way. The sails blew out from under the gaskets. They were nearly new canvas, but they were blown into strips like ribbons. The ship shook with a frightful tremor.

The wind was blowing with such force that the sea could not rise. Instead, it was rolling over with a white foam; and the foam, as it dashed against the weather side of the ship, would send a spray over us like fine, drifting snow.

It was full moon, and that heightened the terror. It made the dangers visible and invisible by turns, for clouds rushed over our heads with frightful rapidity. They were very low — so low it seemed as if we could reach them. They were like frightened spirits fleeing from the wrath of the storm-god !

The cargo was secured with billets of wood, so I had no fears on that score. There was no danger of its shifting. The real peril was the chance of being blown ashore on the coast of

Africa, and losing our lives in the surf; but the wind kept veering and that held us off.

The hurricane increased in fury until the ship was pressed bodily down into the water and held there.

Resolving to make sacrifices to save our lives, I ordered the top-mast back-stays cut away, and when that was done the masts went crashing over the ship's sides, carrying everything aloft with them. They lay thumping against the vessel till I thought they would stave her side in. To prevent this, I ordered all the lee rigging cut away.

The men started from the hurricane-house. Six had knives and axes, and each of them had a rope round his waist. Six others had hold of the ropes, and clung to any stable thing they could reach — some grasping the weather lash-rail, some seizing hold of the sky-light, and one taking a turn round the stump of the mizzen-mast — while the men with the axes and boarding-knives went down the sloping deck; and, standing in water up to their waists, hacked at the rigging. The wind blew so powerfully that it was next to impossible to swing an axe. Most of the work was done with knives.

Even the sacrifice of all three masts seemed to have no effect toward easing the ship. No sooner had my men crawled back under the hurricane-house than a tremendous breaching sea boarded us over the weather side the whole length of the vessel, staving bulwarks and clearing everything off deck — lce boats, craft, oars, everything but our try-works, weather boat and cook's galley.

The hurricane continued with unabated fury until eight o'clock the next morning. Then it steadily died out, and at noon it was nearly calm. But as the wind went down the sea came up. The waves rose to a dizzy height.

Despite the difficulty in keeping our footing — for the ship tossed and rolled helplessly with not a stitch of canvas to steady her — all hands were busy clearing away the wreck, for a tangle of rigging still remained, and there were several spars alongside, though fortunately none of them end-on.

There was a calm for the space of four hours, and during that calm the ship was covered with birds, which had been blown off from the land — gulls, hawks, boobies, parrots, cockatoos, cranes and pheasants — bright-colored waifs, wearied with the storm and so eager for a place to rest that they forgot their natural fears of one another and of human kind. They perched on the tops of the broken masts; they sat upon the dismantled stanchions; they crowded the rail — where any rail remained; they swarmed in a many-tinted flock upon the shattered skylight; they lit upon our heads and shoulders. It was calm because we were then in the centre of a revolving storm. The birds had sought its centre by instinct.

At half-past four the wind began blowing again with terrific force from the west. The starboard rail and the one boat left on the cranes went under water. When the ship began to rise it took the boat off. We had the full power of the hurricane until noon the next day, and all that while we were entirely helpless and lay at the mercy of the winds and waves, all hands aft under the house for safety.

Now, ever since the storm began, my wife and children had been lying below in her stateroom in utter darkness. It was impossible to keep a light burning; and when the mizzen-mast went over the side, it smashed the skylight and we had to batten it down as you do the hatches.

. Every little while I would go below to the cabin and ask Mrs. Robbins if she wanted me to stay with her, but she insisted I must remain on deck.

"We are safe in God's hands," she said, "and He will care for us and do what is best for us all."

Her courage was magnificent. She seemed to have no anxiety for herself. All her fears were for the poor sailors on deck. She urged that I must be there " to save them from being washed overboard."

One of the children, tired and restless from lack of sleep, piped up, " Papa, why doesn't God make the wind stop blowing ? "

Once, when the wind was raging its worst, the second mate came up to me and said, " Cap'n, I must go below — I've taken a terrible tumble and almost broken my back ! "

I knew the man was lying ; but as he was too frightened to be of any use on deck, and as he might possibly be some company for my wife, I sent him below.

There the fellow dropped on his knees upon the cabin floor and began to pray for his " *dear wife at home !*" That was too much for Mrs. Robbins, and she giggled outright.

" Mr. Simpkins," she cried, " it seems to me you'd show more sense to pray for the folks in peril for their lives aboard this wreck, instead of praying for a dear lady seven thousand miles away on dry land ! " After that the officer prayed in silence or not at all.

Ever since the hurricane began, and it had now been raging for forty-eight hours, I had fed my

"THOMAS POPE" IN THE HURRICANE.

men on canned provisions I had brought for the
cabin table. Lucky dogs they were to get a
mouthful! Cooking was out of the question.
But now, as the weather moderated, Mrs. Robbins
came to our relief. With the aid of her little
alcohol lamp she made coffee for those sorry
toilers of the sea — the strongest coffee and the
best, said one and all that had ever been boiled
aboard a wrecked blubber-hunter!

When, at last, the wind hauled to the south and
died away and the tempest was over, we began to
take account of stock. As O'Hoolihan has it, we .
stood off and looked at ourselves. We counted
our bruises.

Merciless Neptune, what a finding! Jib-boom
gone at the cap on the bow-sprit; fore-mast
broken away at the eyes of the rigging, turning
the fore-top over till the cross-trees pointed to the
zenith; main-mast snapped off at the head;
mizzen-mast gone, save a wretched stump about
seven feet tall; bulwarks and rails shattered;
and five of our six boats missing!

What a frightful change had come over that
poor, storm-stricken ship! A handsome, well-
found barky she had been only two days before —
taut and in perfect trim, "man-o'-war fashion,"
as sailors say — but now she was a pitiable,

dismantled wreck, though, thanks to the faithfulness of her builders, her stanch live-oak hull was sound and tight.

That cabin of ours was a sight to behold. It was a week before we could make it a decent place to live in, for everything was drenched with salt water; and the two harness-casks, containing salted beef and pork and pickles, had worked out of their lashings and emptied their savory contents down the sky-light into the cabin. Mrs. Robbins thought it was "much nicer to keep house on land."

But we were safe and sound, every one of us. Even the "injured" second mate, who was obliged to go below on account of the "terrible tumble" he had taken, had now recovered the use of his spine. Furthermore, we were well provisioned. We had food enough and water enough to last us till we could reach some civilized port and refit the *Pope*. It might be a tedious passage, but we had nothing in particular to be afraid of — considering.

So we made the best of a bad matter. We rigged up jury-masts, and in a week's time we were able to set top-sails and courses, jib and spanker.

I was puzzled at first to know what port to make for. If we kept on our course to the

northward, we should have favorable winds; but
I could think of no port in that direction where
we could be sure of getting spars and whale-boats
and rigging. In fact, the only port really to be
considered was Mauritius. So thither we turned,
keeping the ship headed to the southward, and
beat around the south of Madagascar. Forty
days after the hurricane we sighted the Mauritian
harbor of Port Louis. Considering that the *Pope*
was a wrecked ship under frail jury-masts, and
considering also that we had to contend against
rugged weather nearly all the way, I thought that
I had done my duty faithfully and succeeded
triumphantly.

As we were limping into port, Russell came up
to me with an insinuating look in his sly little
eyes. "Cap'n Robbins," he said, "if you will
pardon me, I have something unpleasant to say to
you. I think it only just to myself to insist that
if you had taken my advice we should not now be
putting into Port Louis for repairs!"

"What advice, pray?"

"Why, don't you remember? I mean my
advice about the albatross, of course — the poor,
white murdered albatross. Have you forgotten
that when you insisted upon having that bird
killed I said, ' Cap'n Robbins, we shall all be very
sorry for this?' "

E. D. Ashley

"THOMAS POPE" UNDER JURY MASTS.

" Russell ! " I shouted, forgetting in my amusement to give my mate his " Mister," " what on
earth do you mean by thrusting a lubberly f'c's'le
superstition into the face of the master of a ship ?
Whaling cap'ns don't know — poor, grass-combing
waisters !   But before the mast — oh, that's the
place to look for erudition !   Oh, yes !   *That's* the
place to find the true navigator !   That's the
place, and not the quarter-deck ! "

Russell turned a paler shade of yellow than
usual — he was thoroughly scared.

" But, Cap'n, in justice to myself, I must insist
that the fact about the albatross rests upon
surer ground than any mere fo'c's'le gossip.   I
have it, sir, upon the authority of Coleridge ! "

" Coleridge ! " I bellowed, in a voice that would
have quelled a mutiny.

" Yes, Coleridge."

" *What* Coleridge ? "

" Why, Coleridge the writer."

" Writer on navigation ? "

" No, no, no, of course not.   I mean the writer
of poetry."

" Not Samuel Taylor Coleridge ?   Thunder and
lightning, *what* a first mate!   *Samuel Taylor
Coleridge?*   And you have the lordly impudence
to thrust Samuel Taylor Coleridge into the face

of the master of a New Bedford whaler! By
George, you deserve to be — ! "

But I turned on my heel and trod the quarter-
deck in silence. Already a tug-boat was coming
out to meet us. She came alongside, haggled
as usual, closed the bargain, and took our line.
As soon as we were well under way again, I
approached Russell once more. I tried to acquire
an insinuating, Russell-like look in my own eyes.

" Mr. Russell," I began, " if you will pardon
me, I have something unpleasant to say to you.
I think it only just to myself to insist that, if *you*
take *my* advice, you'll save wear and tear on your
nervous constitution by bidding a fond adieu to
this nonsense. Come! You're an officer now.
Just shake yourself free of the fo'c's'le. And I
tell you, too, Mr. Russell, that it rests on better
authority than Samuel Taylor Coleridge. It rests
on the authority of a good seaman ! " (Laughing
in my sleeve.)

Poor, humiliated Russell! He wriggled in his
roundabout and grew yellower than before. He
looked like a bilious Cape Codder.

" Why, Charles! " called a gentle voice from
the cabin doorway, " you're not going to dis-
charge Mr. Russell because he believes in the
' Ancient Mariner ! ' "

It was my wife. She had been down below, preparing our "long togs" to go ashore, and now she had come on deck just in time to overhear my remarks to Russell.

"Hannah, my dear," said I, "Mr. Russell is by no means discharged. I beg you, don't worry! Mr. Russell is the best mate I ever had in all my sea-faring days, only he's capable of improvement yet. And as for the albatross — his poor, 'murdered' albatross — 'seems to me you've got those wings somewhere, haven't you? Well, we'll make some kind of a feather ornament of them, and hang it up in the cabin, my dear, for a mascot. For if there's any meaning at all in a 'murdered' albatross (which same I gravely doubt) it means that when you've been wrecked in a hurricane out on the Mozambique channel, you get into Port Louis with all hands alive and unhurt! Eh, Russell?"

THE CAPTAIN.

THE Captain does not always talk in the jargon of the fo'c's'le. In fact it might be said he uses it merely when he "spins a yarn" in order to be more realistic. He talks with his family, his friends at home and his townspeople like any well-educated man whose school-days are far behind him, but who has learned more of men and things from cruising about the world than any books could teach. So this last chapter shall be told in the every-day language he commonly uses when in port among his fellow-men.

There are several anecdotes of himself that the Captain has forgotten to relate. Perhaps he did not think them of sufficient importance, but I do, and so will you when I have told them as they were told to me.

The Captain, like many another old salt, loves dearly his country's flag, though he does not say much about it. But he has carried it into too many strange countries and welcomed the sight of it like a friend from home in too many foreign ports not to be fond of it.

Though he never went to war he had an opportunity to defend the flag when it was insulted in an alien country.

13

The Captain used to tell us this story. He said:

"I was seated one day beneath the shade of some great trees in front of an hotel in St. Helena with two other American captains.

"It was very hot and the streets were almost deserted. Nobody seemed to be about. We sat there quietly enjoying ourselves, when we saw three burly-looking sailors coming up the street.

"They belonged on a large English ship that had just anchored in the harbor. They were rough-looking, and evidently meant to make trouble for somebody if they could.

The United States consul's office was exactly opposite us, and of course our flag was flying from a tall staff in front.

"When the sailors came up to it, they began to call out in derision, insulting the stars and stripes. Then they cast off the halyards and hauled it down, cursing in the vilest language the 'bloody Yankee flag,' as they called it, and wrapping it about themselves, trailing it in the dust.

"'We could stand it no longer,' said the Captain. 'We felt it was time we took a hand. So when they began to pitch into the consul's clerk, who came out to try to rescue the flag, we, too laid hold of them and a general fight ensued.

LANDING PLACE, ST. HELENA.

" 'We did not intend to hurt the men, but we did mean to hold them until the police came.

" 'I had my man down and was holding him with both hands when he reached up and grabbed my long whiskers. He had me then completely at his mercy. I could not release myself.

" 'The clerk ran out of the office to relieve me, and in trying to strike down the hands of the man beneath me he gave me a severe blow over my eye with an ebony ruler. It was so sore I had to stay in my room for several days.

" 'The sailors were arrested and fined three pounds each. Their captain paid their fine and the police put them on board their ship.

" 'We found out afterwards that they came on shore with the intention of making a 'row' and getting shut up, hoping their captain would go without them ; but you see their plan did not succeed.' "

It was during the war of 1863 that the Captain was at St. Helena, and he was one day on shore dining at the hotel. There were a number of ladies and gentlemen in the party. Several of the latter were captains of American ships that lay in port.

The Captain said :

" A large English ship had just anchored in the harbor, and her Captain came ashore to take dinner.

" He evidently had left his good manners aboard ship, for he entered the room in a blustering manner, ignoring the ladies present, and seated himself near the head of the table and began to talk to an English officer who was one of the guests, about our Civil War, asking questions in a most offensive manner.

" We were all feeling very much pleased over the news of victory we had received and some one began to tell the captain of Sherman's march to the sea.

" The English captain, whom we afterwards learned was one of England's naval reserves, spoke up in a loud and boasting tone, saying, ' Well, sir, we will go over and heip the Southerners whip the Yankees when we get back to England.'

" Captain Kelley, an American and a man of small statue, was sitting near me, and I noticed his temper was rising. He could not sit still in his chair. As the English captain went on with his boisterous and blustering talk, he jumped to his feet, pushed up his coat-sleeves, looked the Englishman full in the face, and said, ' It is not necessary for you to wait to whip Yankees. Come out into the street and I will give you a chance, for I'm a Yankee.'

"THE BRIARS," ST. HELENA.

"Kelley was about one-half the size of the Englishman, who looked thoroughly ashamed. He made a lame sort of an apology and left the house. He got his supplies on board that very afternoon and sailed that night, so we never saw him again."

"How did I happen to be in St. Helena?" said the Captain.

"It happened this way. We lay in the harbor of Mauritius two months repairing damages, and getting new masts, rigging and sails; but we couldn't get a whaling boat.

"My crew were deserting and good men were hard to obtain in that quarter, so as soon as my sails were ready, I put to sea and finished rigging her. If any whales had come in sight we couldn't have taken them, as we had only one boat.

"After being a month at sea, we spoke the *Plover*, another whaler, and got one old boat from her. So, having now two boats, we succeeded in capturing two whales.

"At the end of six months we put into Port Louis and found four new whale-boats had been sent us. But we were in as bad a condition as before, for now we had plenty of boats and no crew to man them.

"We went to the Seychelle Islands and there I shipped nine men. We cruised in the Indian

Ocean for two years, with poor success, so I decided to head the bark homeward. We had fine weather round the Cape of Good Hope and steered straight for the Island of St. Helena, where we stayed two weeks, so I had a chance to see all there was in that noted place."

St. Helena lies in the track of all vessels bound from Cape of Good Hope to the United States.

" You know, perhaps, that the island is twenty-eight miles in circumference, and is in latitude 15° 55" South, longitude 5° 42" West. It rises up out of the sea like a great tower on the horizon. You can see it forty miles away, a great blur in the distance, on a clear day. As the vessel approaches it, Dana's peak, 2,700 feet high, is first seen above the clouds.

" The island has good anchorage on the north side abreast of Jamestown.

"I took my family on shore and we visited many parts of the island and all the places that are of world-wide interest on account of their connection with the great Napoleon. The Briars, where he lived while Longwood Old House was being prepared for him, was occupied by my esteemed friend, George Moss, Esq. It is situated on a plateau at the foot of the hills and has a fine garden. It is surrounded by wild and rocky scenery. The Briars has always been kept as it was when Napoleon lived there. In one of the rooms it is said that he gave the dictation to ' Las Casas.'

" Longwood Old House was originally a farm-house, but verandas were added and the place otherwise improved. After Napoleon's death the house fell into a state of dilapidation.

" Longwood New House was built for Napoleon, but he never lived in it. It is a one-storied build-ing, and has fifty-six rooms of various sizes.

" It is pleasantly situated in the Eastean part of the island, 1,760 feet above the sea.

" Another interesting building is St. Paul's church, in whose graveyard are buried many strangers who have died on the island.

" Jamestown is in a valley between two lofty hills and is a picturesque spot, with roads winding up the hills on each side.

" Ladder Hill is 600 feet high, and is crowned with a strong fort with barracks for a regiment of soldiers.

" If one wishes to ascend it he may go by the road which winds up the sides of the hill, or, curiously enough, by a long ladder with 365 steps, which reaches from the town at the bottom to the fortress at the top."

Tell us some of your adventures while there, Captain.

"Yes, I think I have given you geography and history enough. But it is pleasant for me to remember I have been in the very rooms where the great Napoleon planned and thought and regretted his life away.

"Our adventures? Well, here's one. The very first day we went ashore we had dinner in Smith's hotel. While we were eating, down came the walls over our heads covering us with plaster.

"No, it wasn't an earthquake, but the work of the white ant which eats up the woodwork of the houses and down they fall when least expected. I tell you, it is dangerous. So some of the dwellings are made of teak wood and the warehouses of iron, both indestructible by this pest.

"We had many drives about the island, visiting Napoleon's grave and drinking from the spring near Longwood, where he walked every day as long as he was able. It is a pleasant spot, cool and shady from the overhanging willow trees.

"Pleasant as was our stay in St. Helena, after our long ocean voyage, we were glad to point the bow of our vessel homeward.

"Yet we were troubled greatly by rumors we had heard of the Confederate cruisers, always

"LADDER HILL" AT ST. HELENA.

ready to pick up vessels belonging to the North, and we kept a good watch out, I assure you, for such cruisers.

"North of the Bermudas we saw traces of the foe in the shape of an abandoned hull, her masts gone, and bearing the marks of fire. We ran near enough to hail her, but no one was on board.

"At last we, too, ran into danger. When only fifty miles south of Nantucket Shoals, our lookout sighted a steamer two points off our lee bow. I went aloft, fearing the worst. My fears were confirmed when I made her out to be a long, rakish, bark-rigged steamer, standing across our bows and heading towards the north.

"I was sure we were lost. But we had suffered all kinds of perils and were to be spared this. For a large ship had been in sight of us all day about eight miles to the windward, steering in the same direction that we were.

"She was a richer prize than we would be, and we saw through our glasses the steamer overhaul her and send a boat to board her.

"It was about sunset when this happened. So we clapped on all sail, put out our lights and sailed away, fearing lest the steamer should take us ; but the next day it was thick and foggy, and we saw the steamer no more.

"About thirty miles south of No Man's Land we fell in with a fleet of fishing vessels and gave them a great fright, for they thought we were the enemy.

"When we lowered a boat to go alongside of them, we could see them pulling in their lines to try to escape us.

"But we soon convinced them we were all right, and exchanged some of our salt pork for a fine mess of fresh mackerel. They told us how the land bore, and the next morning, June 25, at five o'clock, we came to anchor off Butler's flat in the lower harbor, New Bedford.

"We had left St. Helena on the first of May, and it was just three years and eleven months since we had sailed from home on what proved a long, disastrous and unfortunate voyage.

"We had suffered from a severe hurricane, losing our boats, which were not replaced for nearly a year.

"Our officers and crew had deserted us, which completely spoiled our plans.

"Yet our ship was new and well-provisioned, and we were so far from home we could not return.

"We had seen whales enough to overload us with oil, but we could not capture them because we had not men enough to do it.

"Yet, when we got home, oil was so high that what we had brought a good price, so our voyage was a paying one, after all.

"Oh, I must tell you that we found out after we got ashore the vessel that we saw captured was the Isaac Webb of New York, and that after catching her, the steamer tried to find us, but thanks to the fog and our good fortune, she was unsuccessful."

www.ingramcontent.com/pod-product-compliance
Lightning Source LLC
Chambersburg PA
CBHW031954060726
47497CB00016B/2083